THOSE WHO CAME BEFORE

C.L. Sharples

Copyright © 2024 C.L. Sharples

All rights reserved

The characters and events portrayed in this book are fictitious. Any similarity to real persons, living or dead, is coincidental and not intended by the author.

No part of this book may be reproduced, or stored in a retrieval system, or transmitted in any form or by any means, electronic, mechanical, photocopying, recording, or otherwise, without express written permission of the publisher.

ISBN: 9798325405730

*For those who thought their first
love would be their last*

I've been afraid of changin'
'Cause I've built my life around you

                                        FLEETWOOD MAC

CHAPTER ONE

Last-minute packing has never been my thing. Yet here I find myself, launching sweaters and underwear and a maybe-I'll-wear-this-but-I-probably-won't cocktail dress into my suitcase.

There is absolutely no order to it. Zero neatness. If I weren't in such a rush, I'd be itching to organise it, but as it happens, I am rushing. Very much so. This is what happens when you receive a last-minute text from your brother's girlfriend saying your ride will be with you any second now.

My ride, by the way, is a man I'm yet to meet. My brother's girlfriend's brother.

I say I'm yet to meet him, but the truth is, I feel like I know him already. I've heard enough stories about the guy to be able to paint a pretty decent picture. He's twenty-six, one year older than me, and he's the type of brother who would enter a party with a baseball bat if he heard someone was threatening his sister. Terrifying, I know, but also kind of admirable.

He's also the type of person you don't want to keep waiting, hence my current rush.

I hear a knock on the door and try not to shriek. It's followed by the loud *ding-dong ding* of the doorbell. Throwing my suitcase closed, I dive on it, doing my best to squash the contents down so I can pull the zippers together. This is the trouble with packing for a winter getaway: all of my items are bulky.

Once the two zips are at a reasonable distance from one another, I lug the suitcase downstairs, taking care not to topple over with its weight.

"I'm coming!" I call to Adrian, whose name I thankfully remember.

"Don't rush on my account."

"Oh." I stop still when I notice the man standing at the bottom of the stairs. He's tallish, with dirty-blonde, tousled hair, thick brows, and a tan complexion. He looks younger than twenty-six except his jaw looks chiselled with age. He's dressed casually in an oversized hoodie and light-wash jeans, but he manages to pull the look off. Much better than me standing in my oversized sweater and leggings. I trail my eyes upwards, past his Adam's apple, stopping on the bright blue eyes that are now locked on mine.

"Or maybe rush a little."

"Sorry." I drag my luggage down the last few steps, passing him as I enter the living room, where I pause, compelled to turn back. "You have really nice eyes."

He blinks as though he didn't expect me to say that. But really, I'm sure he hears it all the time. They're the kind of cerulean blue that I bet has everyone staring.

"Thanks?" He poses the word as a question, and I can't help but smile.

"You're welcome." Leaving my luggage by the radiator, I head for the kitchen, where I stop again, a sudden thought hitting me. "Wait, how did you get in here? I didn't give you a key."

Adrian pauses by my luggage. He looks wildly out of place in my undecorated, tiny living room, like a fire crackling in a polar desert. "The door was ajar. I thought you left it that way for me."

"Ah, no. That'll just be my dodgy lock."

"You should get that looked at."

"I know." I smile over my shoulder before disappearing into the kitchen. It's as barren as the living room and as shamefully without character. "I'll just be a minute," I call to him. "I'm grabbing the snacks."

Two minutes later, I'm back in the living room, hugging a picnic basket to my chest and staring at this

3

stranger who's staring at my picnic basket like there's a dragon curled up inside.

He sucks in a deep breath. "This is a nice place you've got."

I have a feeling he's going to circle back to the basket. "No, it's not," I laugh. "It's completely void of any personality." His look tells me he knows it's true. "I moved in here earlier this year," I explain. "And I haven't gotten around to doing anything with it yet."

"Why not?"

I shrug as an uncomfortable feeling crawls up my chest. "Honestly? I have no idea how to answer that question."

He stares at me for a few seconds longer before dipping his head at the basket. "Are you going to explain what that's all about?"

I hug the basket a little tighter. It's not like I expect him to try and pry it from me or anything, but if he tells me there isn't enough room for it in the car, I'll put up one hell of a fight. "It's, like, a four-hour journey, isn't it?" I quiz. "We're going to need snacks. And I packed some for you, too."

"Six hours, probably. Given the weather. And thanks. I, er—didn't think to bring any."

My relief that he isn't telling me to leave the basket behind is overthrown by my surprise. "You didn't think to bring food on a six-hour car journey?" As I wait for him to respond, I move to the window, peeping through the blinds to find the sky frosty-blue and clear. "And what's wrong with the weather?"

"There's meant to be a storm later." He runs a hand through his ruffled hair when I turn to face him again. A stray lock tumbles over his brow, but he doesn't seem to notice. "That's why I got here early. I'm hoping we can miss it."

It's only now hitting me that I'll be spending the next several hours with this man whom I barely know, and there'll be little else to entertain us besides each other. "If I annoy you on this journey, please don't tell me."

"I definitely will."

Annoying mode: switched off.

I notice the thin square box in his hands and tilt my head. It's been wrapped in white paper dotted with pastel-coloured presents, and it confuses me enough that I raise a brow at him.

"Oh." He looks down as if just now remembering that he holds something in his hands. "This is for you."

"For me?" My confusion amplifies.

"It's your birthday today, isn't it?"

Entirely surprised that Adrian would gift me something when he doesn't know me, I place the basket down and take it, unsure what to say in return. "Thank you," I go with. "How did you know that it's my birthday today?"

"Your brother told me."

"Right." I look at the gift, a giddy smile forming on my lips. "Can I open it?"

"You probably should. It'll need using up today."

Usually, I don't enjoy opening gifts in front of the giver because I always feel the pressure to react, but when I see what's inside, it's with genuine pleasure that my eyes flick up to meet his. "Japanese mochi?"

"Yeah, er—" He rubs the back of his neck. "Your brother also told me that you love the stuff—"

"I do love the stuff."

"—and I thought you could have it on the journey. But…" His eyes trail to the picnic basket by my feet.

"Oh." I look at it with him. Kicking the basket further away, I say, "Don't worry. This mochi is getting preferential treatment. Have you ever tried it before?"

"No. Never."

"Then you're in for a treat. This is the best dessert in existence."

That earns me a small smile. "Then I'm glad Jordan was honest when he told me what you'd like."

"You didn't need to go to the trouble, though. Really, I appreciate this so much."

He shrugs. "I don't mind shopping for birthdays. It's

Christmas that I hate." I'm about to ask him to elaborate on that, especially with the festive season being in full swing, when he adds, "What's with the bulk, by the way?" and I'm looking down as he nudges my bulging suitcase with the tip of his sock. He's taken his shoes off, I notice for the first time. Very polite. "Didn't my sister tell you we're going for six nights, not six weeks?"

"Warm clothes happen to be bulky."

"Is that so?" His lips twitch. "You don't happen to have packed fifty blankets?"

"My blanket!" Ignoring his look of perplexity, I dart past him, taking two steps at a time up the stairs. In my room, I pull my thick, woollen blanket from my bed, tartan and perfect for winter, before carrying it down to a still-perplexed Adrian. "I need it for the car journey," I explain. "It's cold out there."

He shakes his head, nodding at the other object in my hands. "And the pillow? Is that for warmth, too?"

"Listen." I put on my schooling voice. "When it's the heart of winter, and you're going to a lodge in the middle of the woods, and you have a four-hour—"

"Six."

"—Six-hour car journey ahead of you, these items are essential."

"It isn't *quite* in the middle of the woods." The lodge is Adrian and his sister Evie's holiday home. According to Evie, they've been going to it almost every Christmas, and this year, they were kind enough to invite Jordan and me to join. Well, Evie was kind enough. I'm not sure what Adrian thinks about it. And, if I'm being honest, I'm pretty sure my invite was more of a sympathy thing. "And it'll be more than six hours if we don't get going."

Adrian helps me load my items into the back of his gleaming SUV. It's large enough to hold my luggage comfortably beside his, and if I'd have known that earlier, I might have packed more blankets.

Once the boot is closed, I turn to face him with my hand held out. "I'm Ophelia, by the way."

"I know your name." He shakes my hand with a perplexed expression. "I'm Adrian."

"And I know your name," I smile. "I just thought it would be nice if we officially introduced ourselves. It's nice to meet you, Adrian."

"Well, Ophelia." He leans his hand against the boot of his car. "Ready to hit the road?"

"Absolutely."

CHAPTER TWO

Adrian, I'm finding, is the perfect travel companion.

He's given me complete control over the music, which, in my opinion, makes you undeniably a great person to drive with. And I have the mochi. Could today get any better?

"Mmm." I chomp down on a chocolate-ganache-filled mochi, savouring the chewy outer layer and the melt-in-the-mouth centre. "Mmm," I groan again, sinking back into my seat. "You *have* to try one. Here." I hold one out to him, catching him looking at me with an expression I've seen numerous times already. It's like he hasn't quite figured me out yet but is trying really hard to.

"Alright." He takes it from me, eyeing the mochi ball with narrowed eyes before taking a small bite and chewing tentatively. "What is that?" he asks, pulling a face as he chews some more. "And why is it so chewy?"

"*That* part is the mochi. It's chewy and delicious."

"It's chewy and disgusting." He spits it into a rogue tissue and tosses it on the back seat.

I frown at the side of his face. "I can think of something else that's disgusting."

"Sorry." He wipes his mouth before putting both hands back on the wheel. "I don't usually have people in the car with me." I can see why. "By the way, do you like being called Ophelia? Or do you prefer Phi? Your brother calls you Phi, right?"

"I'm Phi to my brother and Phi-Phi to my mum." I look out the window as I try not to recall the ex-boyfriend who the nickname originates from. He started calling it me nearly a decade ago, and I loved it at the time, but now…

"What should I call you?" Adrian asks.

"Ophelia's fine."

I note how the sky is starting to look gloomier from when we first set off, not only because of the low-sitting winter sun but the thick clouds that seem to be getting heavier.

"Everybody calls me Adrian," he says. "I'm not even sure what they'd call me for short. Aid?"

My lips twitch as I turn to look at him. "But what if people mistake it as a cry for help? Aid! Aid! See how it can get confusing?"

He glances at me with that same look before biting his lip and staring out of his windscreen. A laugh escapes him the next second. "Okay. Yeah. I see what you mean."

Grinning, I tuck myself deeper into my blanket and hum along to Beyonce's *XO*.

"Don't take this the wrong way or anything," Adrian continues, interrupting my rhythm, "but aren't you supposed to be depressed?"

"Depressed?" I twist to face him, taken aback before remembering who he's been talking to. "How much has my brother told you?"

He bites his lower lip. "Not...*much*. Just that the love of your life—or the person you consider to be the love of your life—left you earlier this year, and it broke your heart." He glances at me before darting his eyes back to the road. "Sorry if I'm overstepping."

I examine the side of his face, briefly wondering why it looks so sun-kissed, before saying, "On the contrary, I consider my heart to be very whole."

His eyes fling back to me. I look away, tucking my feet —shoes off—onto the seat. "What do you mean by that?" he asks. "So he *didn't* break your heart? Your brother seems pretty certain that he did."

"I just don't like the term. He *hurt* my heart, sure. But

11

it's still whole. It's still capable of loving deeply and fully. It's just…" I pucker my lips. "Okay, this is going to sound cheesy, and I'd appreciate it if you don't repeat it, but at the moment, it still beats for him."

He doesn't laugh like I thought he might. On the contrary, he looks thoughtful, maybe even a little concerned. "So you're not…you're not depressed, are you? Evie made it clear that I need to be nice to you. Ergo the mochi."

I smile at that. "I have my dark days," I confess. "Jord has seen a lot of those. Evie has, too. But what my brother and your sister don't know is that at the back of every dark day, I have a thousand thoughts spurring me on. They pull me out of it."

"What kind of thoughts? Sorry," he quickly adds, raising a hand from the wheel. "I don't mean to pry. I'm just curious."

"It's okay. I don't mind talking about it. Let's see…" I tap my lip as I stare out the window. "I guess I tell myself it's all part of the process. To hurt is to heal, and I need to allow myself to feel the hurt and not baulk from it if I'm going to heal fully. I tell myself that I'm strong and that what I'm feeling is okay. It's part of being human. I remind myself that to hurt deeply is to love deeply and to love deeply is a strength. I remind myself that I have things to look forward to. Places to see, new people to meet when I get there.

"But mostly," I sigh. "I tell myself that the end of a romantic relationship doesn't mean The End. We both still care for each other. We might root for each other from afar now, but there's something beautiful about that."

"I see." Adrian taps his fingers against the wheel in thought, but he doesn't comment further.

"But then I think about him moving on," I continue, "and I spiral again."

"How do you get out of that?"

"I go to bed and cry," I laugh. "And then I remind myself that I love him and that my love isn't conditional. With or without me, I want him to be happy."

"Sounds mature," Adrian notes. "Most people want their exes to be miserable and regretting their choices."

"I do want that sometimes," I confess, twirling my hands together on my lap. "But when I take my feelings out of it, I realise what I really want is for him to succeed. And if I only loved him because I had him, was it really love?"

"This love you talk about. It sounds...rare. I'm sorry you lost it."

"I never lost it." I shake my head. "That love is mine. I love with the promise of forever. I just happened to be with someone who didn't love the same."

As the car starts slowing, I realise I've talked too much—and confessed too much—for far too long. I clear my throat. "So besides the broken heart, has Jordan told you anything else about me?"

"Just that you're quiet."

We both laugh at how obviously untrue that is.

"I'm usually quiet," I admit. "I'll give him that."

"So why am I getting preferential treatment?"

I purse my lips. "I think I have multiple personalities," I confess. "No—wait. I have one personality, but I share different parts of it with different people depending on how I feel. You get my chatty side," I tease.

"I'm not even going to ask what that means about me." He shakes his head before shifting. "Has Evie said a lot about me?"

"Just that you're an amazing brother who will kick the crap out of anyone who tries to hurt his sister. Which, come to think of it, sounds more like a warning to my brother."

He laughs a little. Shifts some more. "Anything else?"

I lean back, eyeing him carefully as I notice the nervous look in his eyes. "Are you trying to tell me there's something I should know?"

"No. I just…So Evie didn't warn you about me?"

"Warn me? Why would she do that?"

"She warns every female friend about me." He rolls

his shoulders, imitating, *"He's a great brother, but he'd make a shit boyfriend.* I *would* make a shit boyfriend," he adds, almost as an afterthought. "So I guess she's right to warn them. But she never warned you?"

"No."

"Hmm."

As he falls into silence, staring out at the road, I contemplate his words. "What makes you think you'd make a bad boyfriend?"

"Because I have no interest in falling in love."

"Huh." Well, at least he's honest about it. "I wonder why Evie decided not to warn me?"

"That's my point. Unless—" He tilts his head. "Maybe she knew you wouldn't be affected by me. What with…" He waves a hand in my direction. "Your current situation."

"I never said I wasn't affected by you."

His brows lift. "Are you affected?"

"I didn't say that, either."

"A woman who speaks in riddles." He nods and purses his lips. "Got it."

I smirk. "If I were a Batman character, I'd be the Riddler."

"I've never seen Batman."

"*None* of them?" My mouth falls open as he shakes his head. Drawing the blanket nearer to my chin, I bite my lip and say, "You know, that's crazy. You actually remind me of a Batman character. The Joker? You look exactly alike."

"I know who the Joker is, dipshit."

My laughter fills the car. Adrian smiles, shaking his head with a quiet chuckle.

After a moment, he says, "This traffic is getting worse."

I peer through the windscreen, up at the sky. "It's starting to snow." Little white flecks drift towards us, hitting the window before dripping down. "Do you think that's what's causing the traffic? Because we're heading into the storm?"

"Probably." Adrian lifts the handbrake as the car stops. Leaning his elbow against the door, he adds, "But it shouldn't be this bad yet."

A few minutes later, he's switching off the ignition. The heat goes with it. I shiver, pulling the blanket higher. "Aren't you cold?" I ask, noticing how Adrian is dressed in a T-shirt, his hoodie discarded on the seat behind him.

"I'm hot-blooded."

"How nice," I sigh. "I guess that makes me cold." I look out the window, but when Adrian laughs, I glance back. "What?"

"It's nothing."

"Or maybe I'm cold because it's literally freezing out there." I pull out my phone and put directions into Maps. "It says we're still six hours away!" I look at Adrian in horror, hoping he'll tell me that my phone has it wrong. When he doesn't, I complain, "Haven't we been driving for two already?"

He leans toward me, peering at my phone by my shoulder. His breath whispers against my neck. "There's been an accident." Using his fingers, he moves the map upward. "There are red patches everywhere. Shit." Groaning, he slams his head back against the seat.

The shiver that runs through me has his eyes pinging back. "You okay?"

"Just cold."

Chewing his bottom lip, he glances at the cars in front of us before looking back at me. "I think this calls for a pitstop."

He indicates for his car to come off the motorway, and before I know it, we're driving along an A-road, the traffic far behind us.

CHAPTER THREE

I allow myself a moment to acknowledge the strangeness of my predicament.

I thought I was catching a ride with someone I barely know. I never imagined I'd be in a hotel room with him, entirely alone.

Adrian paces the floor before me while I perch on the edge of the only bed. He's speaking to Evie through his phone, and it isn't difficult to guess what she's saying to him on the other end.

"I know, I know," he says, running a hand through his hair. "We'll be there in the morning. It was the only way, alright?" He stops walking, using his hands to accentuate his frustration. "I wasn't about to sit in traffic for who knows how long. At least this way, we can both get some sleep in before setting off at first light. I know. I said I *know*, Evie. God. Ophelia?" He glances at me. "She's fine. No longer shivering." Whatever Evie says next has him rolling his eyes. "Alright." He hangs up.

"What did she say?"

"She's worried about you." He scowls at his phone before tossing it on the bed beside me.

"About me? What's there to worry about? Bed bugs?"

He meets my stare, the scowl still remaining. "She thinks I'm going to try and seduce you. You, me, hotel room? Apparently, she doesn't think you're as immune to me as we initially thought."

I can see where Evie's concern is coming from. Her one and only brother cooped up with her boyfriend's little sister in a hotel room. One of which—me—having zero involvement with the opposite sex for several months, and the other—him—being an objectively attractive man.

But—

The scowl disappears as he tilts his head. "Why are you laughing?"

"Because it's funny, isn't it?"

"Why is it funny?"

I wave a hand between us. "Here we have a girl who doesn't know if she can move on from her previous love and a man who's proclaimed he has zero interest in falling in love at all. I don't think Evie has anything to worry about. Do you?"

He turns his face away with a smile. "No. I guess not."

I lean back so I'm resting against the bed with my feet dangling over the edge. "Your sister must think you're irresistible."

"That's a weird thing to say." Perching on the edge of the bed, he lowers himself so that he rests beside me. "But I am irresistible, you know. I just haven't tried with you."

I turn on my side so that I'm facing him. Up close, I can see how shockingly blue his eyes are, like clear water reflecting a perfect sky above.

My type, if I were to go off the one boy I've ever really fallen for, is dark hair, green eyes, and a height that doesn't tower over me. Adrian is none of those things. Adrian is golden. He's blond hair, pretty eyes, and long limbs. Not my type, but I can see why other girls might find him irresistible.

"Go on then," I dare. "Try and seduce me."

His lips pucker. "I don't think your brother would be very happy with me, would he?"

I turn and smirk at the ceiling, ignoring an unexpected swoop in my stomach. "Your confidence is a major turn-off, just so you know."

He nudges my arm, shifting so he's on his back, too. We're silent for a moment. "Evie wanted me to check into a different hotel room," he tells me. "I told her that I would."

I frown. "That sounds like a waste of money."

"That's what I thought."

"So it's settled." I sit up. "We'll both stay in this room, and neither of us will try to seduce the other. Deal?"

He takes my hand as a means to hoist himself into a sitting position. "Deal."

Our hotel room has little to look at. It's sparse in here, with only a mini-fridge, kettle, and small dressing table.

"So…" He scratches the back of his neck as he stares at the biggest object in here—the bed. "You don't mind sharing this with me? I'd be a gentleman, but I'm not sleeping on the floor."

I give myself a moment to think about whether my intended answer is the truth. Really, I don't mind it at all. I'll be sharing a bed with an attractive man with no intimacy involved and zero risk of intimacy. That to me sounds like an interesting experience. "No. Do you mind sharing it with me?"

He shrugs. "It's just sleeping, isn't it? So long as you aren't a snorer." He pauses. "You aren't a snorer, are you? Because if you are, you're out in the hall."

I laugh. "No, I'm not a snorer." After a moment's thought, I quiz, "And if I had minded the bed-share? Where would you have slept then?"

He thinks about it for a moment. Tapping one of the

pillows behind us, he says, "Here. I would've let you take the floor." He stands, examines the room for a moment and looks back at me. "I don't know about you, but I'd rather not be stuck in here for longer than we need to be. You coming for a drink?"

Realising that I'd prefer not to be left alone in this empty hotel room and that a drink with him sounds like a bonding experience, I follow him to the door, grabbing the keycard on my way out.

The lobby is decorated with wreaths covered in holly and festive lights. At the centre sits a glimmering Christmas tree bedazzled in what must be a hundred different baubles. By the seating areas, indoor firepits emit licks of heat, and staff members walk to and from with Santa hats bobbing on their heads.

I ogled at all of this on the way in, but it doesn't stop me from ogling again as we make our way to the door, even if I have to race after Adrian because he doesn't seem to care for the festivities as much as me. His long strides wait for no one.

Outside is even better. The December night sky looks bright thanks to the Christmas lights spreading from one side of the hotel to the other. The hedges are also alight with twinkling fairy lights, guiding our way as we head for the onsite bar. It's a good thing, too, since the snow makes it difficult to see where the path ends and the road starts.

"Don't you just love hotels at Christmas?" I call, having to jog to catch up with Adrian, who seems determined to get to the bar before another minute passes. "They're so festive. It makes everything look magical. Don't you think?"

"Haven't noticed."

"You haven't noticed the Christmas decorations that literally surround us?"

"No." Adrian has his hands shoved deep into his pockets, eyes ahead, and if I shoved a dancing reindeer in front of his face, I get the feeling he'd look the other way.

We enter the pub. The first thing I notice, of course, is that it's decorated in the same festive cheer as the hotel. The second thing is that Adrian walks right past it all like it's just an inconvenience.

Does it dampen my mood a little? Yes. But they also have Christmas music playing in the background, so that cheers me back up again.

"I forgot what places can be like at this time of year," Adrian mutters.

I choose to ignore his negativity as I smile at the barman. "Okay, so this might sound a little strange, but bear with me. I'll have a white Bacardi, with a splash of blackcurrant squash, mixed with water, please."

He gives me a funny look. "That's not strange at all."

As the barman turns to make my drink, I find Adrian staring at me like I'm not just strange, but I'm from another planet.

"What?" I ask.

"I'm going to need you to explain that drink."

"It's ingenious, really. It tastes just like squash with the added benefit of it getting you drunk. *And* the water helps with the hangover."

As the barman pushes the drink to me, Adrian says, "Make it two."

With our drinks in hand, we hunt for a table. Unfortunately, we have very different opinions on where we should sit. I want to be close to the action, where the merry-goers are—those belting out Christmas songs and dancing. Or, if not that, then at least by the fire.

Adrian, on the other hand, walks past it all, his face set like a stone as someone tries to clink glasses with him. I don't protest as we sit in a quiet corner. I think he hates the noise more than I dislike the inaction.

"Oh, this is my favourite Christmas song," I say, hearing *2000 Miles* playing in the background. A slight frown appears on Adrian's face as he stares at his glass. "Do you have a favourite?" I probe.

"No." Downing his drink in one, he stands, stalking

over to the bar without another word.

I frown as I watch him. Isn't he the one who wanted to come here? So why the mood? Clearly, something is bothering him, but I don't know him well enough to know what that something is.

For the next thirty minutes or so, I sip my drink while carefully analysing him, noticing how his eyes avert the decorations, how his frown deepens whenever the music gets too loud, and how he literally flinches when the words "Merry Christmas" are uttered by anyone in the room.

"So what's with you and the holidays?" I feel compelled to ask.

He startles, looking at me like I've exposed something he thought well hidden. "I—what?"

"You and the holidays. What's up with it?"

Again, his mouth works like he's struggling to find the words to say. "Evie didn't tell you?"

I frown at what he's chosen to settle with. "Tell me what?"

"I—It doesn't matter." He turns his face away.

"Go on—you can tell me. Evie will probably do so herself when I see her tomorrow, anyway." I watch his face as he stares resolutely away from me. What could possibly have happened to make him dislike the holidays this much? "Did an ex-girlfriend break your heart during the holidays or something?" I ask the question softly, but his face hardens into stone.

"Drop it."

Thinking I've probably guessed right—and that it explains his adversity to falling in love—I add, "I'm sorry you've been through something like that. But is it really worth losing the Christmas spirit over?" I place my hand over his, hoping to comfort him—after all, this is a shared experience—but he draws his hand back as though my touch is poison.

"I said, *fuck off*." His chair scrapes as he stands, and I watch, startled, as he stalks to the men's room.

My face heats.

"Hey, love, why don't you crack a smile?"

Tearing my eyes from where Adrian disappeared, I find two men walking past my table, drunken eyes on me.

I know I should let it go. I know I should allow them to walk past with no further words spoken, but if there is one thing that gets my back up when it comes to strangers, it's being told to smile.

"Excuse me?"

One of the men places his hand over his heart like I've just spoken the f-word to him. "I was just saying that you should smile more. It will make you look nicer."

"And who said I want to look nice?"

"Woah, woah." He holds his hands up like I've verbally attacked him. "No need to get upset about it."

"Really?" I get to my feet, feeling a rare flare of anger. Unfortunately, this is the moment when Adrian decides to reappear from the bathroom.

He stops still. Eyes flicking between us, I have the wild thought that he's about to join the other side, given what he'd said to me mere minutes ago, but his earlier anger no longer seems to be directed at me.

It takes one second. One second—and he's in the face of the first man, arm pinning him to the wall.

"What did you say to her?" he growls.

"Woah, man." The man holds up his hands, staring at Adrian with wide eyes. "Let's take it down a notch."

"What did you say?" Adrian repeats, shoving him a little harder.

"*Adrian*," I try to plea, but my voice may as well be part of the Christmas music for all he listens to it.

"All he did was tell her to smile," the second man says, looking as surprised as me as he tries to calm the situation.

Adrian turns to face me for affirmation. It's the wrong move. With his attention away, the man manages to shove his way free, straightening his jacket before launching a landing blow onto Adrian's jaw.

The force of it has Adrian falling onto his ass.

"Oh, my God." Racing towards him, I crouch by his side, feeling my heart in my throat. "Are you okay?"

Adrian's eyes are thunder as he rubs his jaw and glares at the two men. Recognising that look as someone about to engage in a fight, I place my hands on his shoulders. "No, no, no. *Nooooo*. No fighting. Please?" I shake him until he looks at me. "Please?" I repeat.

Slowly, the storm clears from his eyes. I drop my hand to his elbow. Part of me expects him to throw it away, but instead, he takes one, two, three quick breaths.

"Alright?" I ask, scanning his face for signs of injury, his body for signs of wooziness. Apart from the bloodied lip, he seems okay. Still, I want to thwack the men myself for doing this to him, although they seem to have had the good sense to leave us.

"I'm fine." He brushes my hands away as he gets to his feet. Together, we leave the bar, Adrian with his eyes downcast, me giving a look to those who dare to stare at him.

"Hopefully we don't see those men when we leave tomorrow," I say as we trudge back through the snow.

Adrian doesn't reply. He's silent, the only sound the crunch of snow beneath our feet.

When we reach the hotel room, he sits on the edge of the bed, staring into nothing.

It unnerves me. I don't know him well enough to

know how he's feeling or what he might be thinking. He may as well be a man sculptured from stone.

My eyes move to his lips, to the congealing blood that proves he's a man of flesh. A man who's probably annoyed at me for two things: first, for pushing him too far when he told me to drop it, and second, for basically being the cause of his injury.

I move to my suitcase. Since there's little else I can do for him but something physical, I pull out my first-aid kit—the one I carry with me on every trip—and walk back to his side.

I hesitate before him. His eyes are no longer latched onto nothing but are focused on the kit in my hand.

"You packed a first-aid kit?"

"You never know when you might need a plaster." I crouch to his level. Inspecting his blooded lip requires touching him, but he doesn't flinch or pull away as I gently hold his face, turning it to the side. My fingers graze his jawbone, seeing the faint bruise blooming there.

"You're a messy packer," he notes.

My face heats as I realise his eyes are now on the suitcase I left open. "Don't," I say. "That's been making me itch ever since we left my house. It's only like that because I didn't want to keep you waiting."

"Oh." He falls back into silence. This close, I can see

the slight crease knotting between his brows, and that, coupled with the blood on his lips, makes me choke, "I'm sorry."

The frown deepens. "*You're* sorry?"

His tone confuses me. "Yes. Why does that surprise you?"

"Because I have no idea what you have to be sorry about. And I've been sitting here trying to figure out how I should apologise to you."

That catches me by surprise. "Why are you sorry?"

"Because I was an asshole to you earlier. I told you to fuck off."

"No." I shake my head. "I took it too far. You told me to drop it, and I didn't. You're not an asshole for setting boundaries."

"I still shouldn't have spoken to you like that. You asked me a question that anyone would have asked. My response wasn't normal."

I stare at him for several seconds, trying to think how best to respond. "Adrian," I start. "For a lot of people, Christmas is the best time of the year, but for some, it's the hardest. I get that. Your response was normal to you. It's okay to feel how you feel. I should have respected that you didn't want to speak about it with me. I forgive you for telling me to fuck off when I didn't."

Adrian's eyes flicker across my face. His throat bobs.

With my hand still gently holding his chin, I feel the motion beneath my fingers, and it awakens something in me. A sense of intimacy that feels too real.

I drop my hand. "Will you forgive me for getting you into a fight?"

"No, no," he quickly protests. "No way do you get to apologise for that. That fight was on me, not you. I got hit because I was an idiot who couldn't control his anger." When my lips curl into a smile, he adds, "You're not going to argue with me on it?"

"Actually, I agree with you. I never would have asked you to pin that guy to the wall. I hate violence."

"Is that why you sounded like you'd swallowed a dog toy when you asked me to stop?"

I give him a grimace before carefully sweeping antiseptic over his cut. "Exactly. Violence—" I shake my head. "I can't bear the thought of someone I care about getting hurt."

"Did you just admit to caring about me, Ophelia?"

My lips curl up. "I suppose I do care about you. A little. You are Evie's brother, after all. And you aren't half bad." As an afterthought, I add, "I also find it impossible not to care about someone I've spent half a day with."

"I get that about you."

My smile deepens when I realise something about him.

"What?" he asks.

"Nothing. Just a thought."

"What thought?"

"That you must care a little bit about me, too." I wipe beneath his lip. "Otherwise you wouldn't have jumped to my defence like you did."

"On the contrary, I jump to people's defence all the time."

"I get that about you."

His smile joins mine.

After I finish cleaning him up, we take turns in the bathroom, and I climb into the bed, pulling the cloud-like quilt to my chin as I wait for Adrian to join me.

He climbs on top of the quilt.

"You're not coming in?" I ask.

"Run hot, remember?"

"Oh." I take a steadying breath as I turn to face the ceiling. Being alone with him like this—in a hotel bed—makes my stomach twist in a way I don't understand. I thought I'd be fine with it, but…it almost feels like I'm doing something wrong.

But I'm not doing anything wrong, and I have no reason to feel guilty. I know that. Yet…I haven't been in bed with a man since the one I shared with my ex-boyfriend, and before that, never.

I look at Adrian, feeling the sudden need to confess

this to him. To get a second opinion.

But he's switching the lamp off, and I'm saying goodnight.

CHAPTER FOUR

Adrian

After freezing my ass off for a solid hour, I finally decided to get inside the quilt.

Ophelia didn't budge. She's still sound asleep, her breathing deep and steady, face peaceful in its slumber.

I keep finding myself looking at her if only to remind myself that this is actually happening—that I'm sharing a bed with a girl, and we won't be having sex.

It's not exactly an unpleasant experience, but it is unusual to feel the warmth of her body beside mine, fully clothed. Hence why I tried staying on top of the quilt for as long as possible.

Thankfully, the words *run hot, remember?* seemed to work on her. Otherwise, she might've insisted I get inside the quilt earlier, and doing this while we're both awake is a step I'm not willing to take.

My lips pull up as I remember what she'd said back in the car. *I guess that makes me cold.* The thought of my blood running hot and hers cold is absurd. The idea of her being anything other than warm is too baffling to believe.

I haven't known Ophelia for long, yet I already know she's one of the good ones. Decency oozes out of her. Her ex must be a real jackass to treat her how he did. She might claim he's this incredible guy—and she clearly, for whatever reason, still loves him—but if there's one thing I know, it's that he doesn't deserve it.

Jordan gave me the full back story on him. Things I doubt Ophelia would ever tell me herself since she seems determined to paint him as a pretty flower. He was ruthless to her after the breakup. Borderline cruel. And all that after spending years promising her his future.

At least I don't allow things to get that far. I know I don't want a girlfriend, never mind a wife, and I make that clear from the start. Those who get involved with me don't end up bruised because of broken promises and built-up dreams. I make sure of that.

Ophelia makes a noise in her sleep, and I peer down to see her smacking her lips together twice before smiling.

Blood rushes between my legs as my dick hardens. I freeze, as equally surprised by my sudden turn-on as I am by its cause. There's nothing I can do but wait for it to go down. No—to *will* it to go down and stop behaving like there's anything here to react to. Taking one, two, three deep breaths, I pray for the moment to pass and for Ophelia not to choose now to awaken.

She makes the noise again—a sound that tells me she's content—and moves so that she's on her side with her arm drooped over me.

Could this get any worse?

My dick hardens again, and I hold back a frustrated sigh as I lay helplessly with little options to choose from. If I wake her, she might see for herself the evidence of her effect. If I do nothing, I'm stuck here with this girl nuzzling into my shoulder with a raging boner that has zero right to exist.

I choose option three: slamming my eyes closed, I imagine the world ending, puppies dying, and wildfires spreading.

Floods.

Tsunami's.

Death.

"Oh."

Hearing Ophelia, my eyes shoot open, landing on hers. She stares up at me with a confused, sleepy expression—one that grows increasingly embarrassed.

If it weren't for the boner that still refuses to go down, this might be comical. Here Ophelia finds herself, waking up with her arm draped over my frozen body, basically drooling onto my shoulder.

"Oh," she says again, jerking back. She raises herself into a sitting position, smoothing her bedridden hair before pulling the quilt up to her chin. "Sorry about that. I'm guessing it was me who snuggled into you since you look like a captive who's been held against his will."

"Don't worry about it." I feel ridiculous, utterly ridiculous, to be lying down while she's sitting upright, but if I move, I'm afraid she'll see what's going on below.

Too. Fucking. Late.

Her eyes widen on my boner before shooting to the ceiling. "Sorry," she says again. "I don't know why I looked there."

I almost laugh.

"No. I'm the one who's sorry. I didn't mean to have, er —" I stop talking.

She shakes her head. "You don't need to apologise to me for being human. I know all about men and their morning glory. You have nothing to be sorry for."

My shame somewhat weakens, but this isn't exactly the type of morning glory she's referring to. If she knew it was caused by her, not some innocent dream, I'm sure she'd be feeling different.

"Well, I'll, um—" She stands, a faint blush appearing on her cheeks. "I'll go use the bathroom while you, er, you know." She waves a hand, darting to the bathroom door, where she pauses. "Do you, um, need any tissue?"

It takes me a second to realise what she's asking. My immediate reaction is to say no, but when I open my mouth, the word "yes" comes out instead. I'm glad she isn't looking when she throws me a wad of toilet roll because it's my cheeks that have now decided to burn. But as awkward as this is, Ophelia has a strange way of making it less so just by being understanding about it.

My dick throbs.

I look down. I haven't been this turned on since...I can't even think of a time.

But when I close my eyes, it's the smell of citrus that hits me. A girl sitting in the passenger side of my car, wrapped in a blanket. A girl with her head on my shoulder.

Shit.
An earthquake.
A tsunami.
Dying dogs.
An earthquake.
A tsunami.
Dying dogs.

I think the images over and over, relieved when it helps, even if there is a dull ache in the aftermath. It's going to be uncomfortable, but I'd rather this discomfort than the one I'd feel if I had to look Jordan in his eyes, knowing I tossed off to his sister.

"Can I come back in?" Ophelia calls from the bathroom. "It's just—I forgot to bring in my washbag."

"I'm done." I grab a wad of toilet roll so it doesn't look like I've failed and push the quilt away from me, twisting so I'm sitting at the edge of the bed.

Ophelia enters the room, and the blaze returns to my cheeks. Forget Jordan—how would I be able to look *her* in her eyes.

Lowering my gaze, I stand, sweeping past her and ignoring the citrus scent that I'm sure to dream about later. When I come back into the room, she has a small bag in her hands, and she's standing in the middle of the carpet like she has something to say to me.

"I'm really sorry about the cuddle thing," she starts. "If I've made things awkward between us—"

"You haven't made things awkward," I assure her. "Besides, getting cuddled isn't the worst thing. You could have done much worse."

That earns me a smile. "Just don't tell Jordan about it, okay? He'd never let me live it down."

"Trust me, Jordan is the last person I'll tell about

this." I walk towards her, towards my suitcase, and pause before I reach it. "So long as you don't tell him about my, you know…"

She laughs. "Yeah, that would be a fun conversation to have with my brother. By the way, Jordan, did you know that Adrian had a raging boner this morning?" She scrunches her eyes closed, cringing. "Sorry."

"Did you have to call it raging?" I complain.

"Sorry. But it did look kind of—" She cuts herself off, cringing again. "Sorry."

I run my eyes across her reddening face with building amusement. "How many times do you normally apologise in a morning? Or is this a record?"

She opens her mouth as if to apologise again but manages to keep it at bay. With a small smile, she says, "Okay, okay. How about we make a deal? I won't tell Jordan about you, and you won't tell him about me."

She holds out her hand.

I take it without hesitation, feeling a *zing* at the touch. "Can we also include Evie in that equation?"

"Please."

I smirk. "Then it's a deal."

As she lowers her hand, she adds, "Should we keep yesterday's incident between us, too? The fight at the bar?"

"Ah." My lips jut into a pucker. Although it looks

nowhere near as bad as it should, I'm praying I can pass the cut off as something else to my sister. "Yeah, I think Evie will tell me off if she hears about that." Ophelia laughs, and I tilt my head as I watch her mouth relax into a smile. "And all because of this." Without thinking, I touch the back of my forefinger to her lips, feeling that *zing* again.

She seems momentarily surprised by the action. But then, as easy-going as anyone I've ever met, she rolls her eyes and says, "You got punched in the face because I wouldn't smile. Happens all the time."

I claw my hand back. "First time for me."

As her smile lingers, a shot of pleasure rushes through me because unlike those assholes last night, I didn't have to ask for it.

"At least your lip isn't looking too bad today," she says, focussing on my mouth. "The cream I used was magic."

So were her fingers as she helped me clean up.

I clear my throat. "We should get ready to leave."

As we walk through reception, I notice how Ophelia offers a smile to everyone, but how she also seems withdrawn, like she'd be happy to talk if anyone approached her, but she wouldn't be the one to start the conversation.

She'd told me yesterday that she'd find it hard not caring about someone she's spent half a day with. At first, I thought that meant she must care for a lot of people—she seems like the type—but as she stays close to my side, I wonder how many people have gotten to spend half a day with her. If I'm one of the lucky ones.

"Do you think we'll be snow-trapped?" she asks after we're checked out and heading outside. "The storm turned pretty brutal yesterday. Just think, we might have to relive this morning all over again."

"This is England," I say as I hold the door open for her. "There's probably a heatwave." Sure enough, the snow has melted into a slush beneath the low-morning sun, but it's still cold enough for Ophelia to shiver.

"No snow day for us," she says, rubbing her arms as we walk to my car. Once inside, I crank up the heating and throw my jacket onto the backseat, Ophelia wrapping herself in that blanket she brought.

We whizz down the A-roads with no traffic in sight. Ophelia remains quiet, almost subdued, as she stares out the window. A couple of times, she opens her mouth as if to say something to me, but she never does. I fight back the urge to ask her to spit it out. If she wants to say something, she'll either do it in her own time or not at all.

As we pass a sign that reads *Sheringham Park*, she finally says it. "I haven't had sex in almost a year."

I make a spluttering noise that I somehow manage to

turn into a cough. She looks at me as though waiting for me to say something back, but really, what the hell am I supposed to say to that?

I pull on the collar of my shirt before cranking the heating down. "Er—"

"Sorry." She looks at her legs, a frown forming.

It's the troubled look that makes me want to say something, to ease her discomfort, even though I have no idea how to deal with things like this.

"You know," I say, "if you're saying that because you want it with me, your timing is kind of off."

Slowly, her lips crack into a smile. "Right," she laughs and leans her head back. "The hotel would have been perfect. Damn it."

"We could still do it at the lodge," I offer. "But I don't think Jordan would appreciate that. I like it noisy."

"Stop," she grins, shaking her head at me. "That's not why I said it."

"So why did you say it? It's alright. I might not be the best at giving advice, but I'm a good listener."

She sighs, the frown reappearing. "Last night..." She tilts her head, contemplating her words. "Last night, when I was in bed with you, I felt...guilty about it."

"Guilty?" Now it's my turn to frown. "We didn't even do anything. What's there to feel guilty about?"

"Nothing. And that's my point. We did nothing, yet

it felt wrong to be sharing a bed with you. Like I was betraying my ex."

"Your ex?" She's lost me. "You mean the guy you're no longer with—the one you owe zero loyalty to?"

"Yes." She sighs. "I know how ridiculous it sounds. Eight months on, and I still feel loyal to him. But I think…I think it's because…Because I've only ever had sex with him before."

I gasp. I know it shouldn't be shocking to me, but the reality is that I haven't met many adult women—if any—who have only had sex with one person before. I can't comprehend it. But I suppose…I suppose I can understand why it must be difficult for her to open herself up to someone new in that way when she's only ever done it with one person.

Sharing a bed with her last night is starting to feel really fucking monumental.

"I guess it feels like…like if I do have sex with someone else, then it really is over. Because for me to have sex with someone, it has to mean something. And if it means something…"

"Then you would have had to have moved on."

"Exactly."

I nod. Although I'm a far cry away from being in her situation, I get it. "So—what?" I shift to face her. "You're holding out on having sex in the hopes that it'll postpone the inevitable?" I know for a fact that her ex isn't doing the same. From what Jordan said, he started dating someone two weeks after breaking up with her.

"Postpone the inevitable." She laughs a sad sound. "That is what I'm doing, isn't it?" We pass the tall, thin trees that mark the start of the forest, their leaves swaying gently above. "It's not like I haven't tried to move on," she continues softly, eyes still downcast. "But whenever I feel physically attracted to someone—or whenever anyone shows an interest in me—I feel this tightness in my chest like I want to run away."

With one hand on the wheel, I lean my elbow against the door, frowning in thought.

Yesterday, I told Ophelia that the love she describes sounds rare. It also sounds fucking painful, which is the exact reason why I don't want it.

"It doesn't have to mean anything, you know," I say. "Sex can be fun when it's meaningless."

She purses her lips. "I respect that, but I don't think it's for me." After eyeing me for a long second, she asks, "Have you ever had it when it does mean something before?"

"No." My answer is immediate, which doesn't surprise me. I haven't.

"Why not?"

I don't want to tell her I'm looking at the reason. "Like

I said. Fun."

"I don't think I could do it." She shakes her head. "I don't think I'd want it."

The thought of her hooking up with some random guy she barely knows doesn't sit well with me, which makes zero sense because why should it matter?

"Then don't." I clear my throat when she looks at me in surprise. "I mean, you've waited this long, haven't you? Why not wait a little longer? If you want it to mean something, wait for it to mean something." I guess that puts me off the table.

She nods. "I'm just afraid I won't find someone it can be meaningful with. It's not just that I'm afraid to move on," she quickly explains. "It's that I'm not sure there is anyone else out there for me. But what's the point of getting with someone else if it's just for the sake of it?"

"Some people enter relationships because they can't be alone," I say. Then, as an afterthought, "I'd rather be you."

She sighs. "Let's not tell Jordan about this conversation, either. Okay?"

I give her my best affronted expression. "What do I look like to you? A common gossip?"

She lightens up after that, but the closer we get to the lodge, the more the cloud shifts over to me. I can't distract myself any longer. Not when we turn onto the familiar dirt road that leads to the park, and I feel the lump forming in my throat, right on schedule.

"This place is beautiful," Ophelia gasps. I keep my eyes ahead, my grip tightening on the wheel. "Look at all of this woodland."

"Mmhmm." Our lodge is two turns from the reception. I know it like the back of my hand, could probably navigate it in the dark.

The familiar nausea begins to climb my stomach the further I drive. I rub my chest, but it does nothing to ease the tightness.

Six years we've been coming here without her. Six years, and it still hits me like it did the first time.

"Are you okay?" I hear Ophelia ask. I can feel her eyes on me. Since having her in the car, I've somehow managed to forget why we were making the journey in the first place—and why I was opposed to having her and her brother come along.

But now the lodge is in view, and I'm pulling up into our lot, wondering why the fuck this girl is sitting beside me.

I switch off the ignition. Evie appears at the door in her winter slippers, Jordan not far behind her. And behind him—something that turns my anger into boiling, irrational rage.

CHAPTER FIVE

I have never been to a place more beautiful than this before.

We're surrounded by trees, so many trees, the tall, thin kind whose wispy tips seem to pierce the sky. The lodge is nestled between them, made from wood so it looks like it sprouted straight from the earth.

When I tip my head back, I can see the early afternoon sky, wintry and crystal clear, glistening through the gaps in the trees as pine needles fall to my feet.

An appeased sigh escapes me. I look toward the lodge, finding my brother and Evie standing by the open door with a smile on their faces.

"You're letting out the cold," I call before smirking at Adrian, who knows all about my aversion to anything anti-warm. Instead of looking amused, like I thought he would, his face looks...livid.

What. On. Earth?

Before I can ask him about it, I'm pulled into a ferocious Evie-hug, the kind that knocks the air from your lungs. "I'm so happy you're finally here!" she squeals, squeezing me tighter.

"Thanks," I choke. "But you're kind of cutting off my windpipe."

"Sorry." She steps back, beaming eyes scanning my face as she holds me at arm's length. "Happy birthday for yesterday. I'm sorry I didn't get to say it in person."

"It's fine." I glance at Adrian, who still has a scowl on his face, and wonder if I'd imagined the smiles he'd given me. "I had fun."

"How was the journey?"

"I thought it was good." Again, I glance at Adrian, who seems set on looking as gloomy as possible while letting me do the talking. Is this somehow part of an act? Is he pretending to dislike me so Evie doesn't think he tried anything on? "How were your few days here without us?" Jordan and Evie arrived three days ago. I could have come with them, but I had work to finish off, as did Adrian.

"We've had an amazing time." Evie leans sideways to look at her brother. "What happened to your lip?"

I turn to look at Adrian with her. His lip really isn't

that bad anymore, but of course his sister would notice it.

He gives her a grimace in answer.

"Alright, sis?" Jordan asks as he wheels by with my luggage. "Adrian," he nods.

Either my brother and Evie haven't noticed Adrian's gloomy mood yet, or they're so used to it that it doesn't faze them, which is odd since this is the first time I'm seeing it, and it is definitely obvious.

Evie loops her arm through mine and moves us towards the lodge. "Was my brother nice to you?"

"He was." I lower my voice to make sure he can't overhear me. "But I'm not sure why he's in a mood now."

"He's always like this when he first gets here."

"But why?"

I'm not even sure if Evie hears me. She's too busy skipping into the lodge in excitement. As I follow her inside, the first thing I think is, *Wow. This is gorgeous.* The second thing is, *Oh, shit.*

My panicked eyes move to Adrian. This, I am pretty sure, is why his mood has turned sour.

"I thought we agreed to no decorations?" he asks.

Evie's lips jut into a pout. "But it isn't just us this year, Adrian. We have Jordan and Ophelia here, too. We can't condemn them to our no-Christmas rule at Christmas."

Adrian's jaw ticks. "You couldn't have warned me?"

"You would have been against it. Besides, I honestly thought when you saw it, you'd love the surprise." When her brother says nothing to that, Evie's eyes flicker to me and away again. "And Ophelia needs cheering up this year."

I wince. She's going to try pinning this on me.

But...When I think about it, I'm glad she's decorated the place. It's festive and cosy, with a wreath hung over the fireplace, tinsel on the windowsills, candles flickering on the table, and gold stars dangling from the ceiling. The only thing missing is a tree.

Why wouldn't you want this?

But I haven't forgotten Adrian's reaction at the pub. He has an adversity to Christmas, and while I don't know why that is, I do know that this has royally pissed him off.

"I like it," I say, hoping to diffuse the situation.

Evie beams, but Adrian aims his glare at me. "Then I hope you enjoy it since I didn't agree to you coming here, either." With that, he turns, taking his bags into one of the rooms off the hallway and slamming the door behind him.

My mouth hangs open.

I guess that marks the end of our short-lived friendship.

It was nice while it lasted.

"I'm sorry about him," I hear Evie say. "Please don't take offence. He's always like this."

I turn to face her. "It's fine. It isn't for you to apologise for."

Jordan appears by her side with more of my luggage in his hands. "I take it he didn't approve of the decorations?"

"No, he did not." Evie's lips pull down. "Will he ever move on? I'm tired of not celebrating Christmas."

"Move on from what?" I ask. I picture an ex-girlfriend of Adrian's, someone who broke his heart on Christmas day or something like that, but didn't he say that he's never had anything meaningful before? How can his heart have been broken if it's never experienced love?

Evie blinks. "It doesn't matter. Come on, let me give you a tour."

The lodge is spacious. It has three bedrooms, two bathrooms, a kitchen, a dining area, and a living room. The last three are all one open space, separated from the bedrooms found in the hall. Jord and Evie have the double room with an ensuite, Adrian has the second double with no ensuite, and I have the twin. Also no ensuite. The bathroom I'll be sharing with Adrian has a walk-in shower, a large mirror, and, thankfully, some air freshener.

"It's gorgeous," I say, following Evie back into the

main living space. There are windows on every wall, and through each one, a breathtaking view of the trees outside.

"If we're lucky, we'll see the deer passing by our window."

They show me the outside next. The lodge has a little seating area on the deck, which would be great for summer but not so great for winter. There's an onsite restaurant, café, and a bar where we can find entertainment and shelter if we want it.

"We can also catch the train into town," Evie says. "It's a cute little place by the sea with loads of independent stores."

"Or there's the village at walking distance," Jordan adds. "Great pub."

"Of course you mention the pub," I smirk. I run my hand across a wooden signpost that reads, *Star Gazing, 200 Yards*. "What's this?"

Evie's smile turns reminiscent. "That's the coolest thing on this park. It's a dark area out in the fields where there's no light to disrupt the brightness of the stars. A place for stargazers. Mum loved it."

"Your mum?" It occurs to me that I've never heard Evie talk about her mother before. "Where is she?"

"Dead," she answers as though she's said the word enough that it no longer affects her.

"Oh." My eyes flick to Jordan and back again. "I'm so sorry."

Jordan gives me an apologetic smile. "I'm sorry, too. I probably should have mentioned that to you."

You think?

"It's okay," Evie assures us. "I've had ten years to process and be okay with it. I was thirteen at the time. I think that's why Adrian finds it so much harder than me. He was sixteen and suddenly hit with so much loss and responsibility. He got a job not long after she died, and as soon as he turned eighteen, he became my legal guardian."

My heart suddenly aches for the boy who drove me here. The same boy who's locked himself away in his room.

"Mum used to bring us here every Christmas," Evie continues. "It was just the three of us, but we loved it. It was only when Adrian turned twenty that he agreed to come back. We've spent it here ever since, but as you can see, he comes here to mope, not celebrate."

Jordan rubs her arm. "That must be hard for you."

"It is!" She shakes her head. "I get it. I do. This is hard for him. But it's hard for me, too, you know? I think Mum would've wanted us to celebrate Christmas. Not skip over it like it doesn't exist."

I think she's probably right. But that doesn't make it

easy.

"So is that why he hates Christmas?" I ask. "Because he misses your mum? Not because..." I trail off as I remember what I'd said to him at the pub. How I'd assumed it was over an ex-girlfriend, and how I'd dismissed that theory later on after hearing he'd never been in love before.

It never occurred to me that the hurt he feels might be due to a different kind of love.

"Our mum died on Christmas Eve," Evie says quietly. "That's why he hates it."

Oh. My. God.

I am such a terrible person.

"Well, I'm here now," my brother says to Evie, wrapping his arm around her shoulders. "And even if we have to celebrate Christmas in secret, we'll still celebrate it."

"Thanks," she laughs, but it's a teary sound.

I get it now. Why Adrian's mood had changed when we got here. And, if I'm honest, I don't blame him for it. He *should* have been warned about the decorations. Especially if it was his first time seeing them up since they came here with their mum. While she probably would want them to continue celebrating the holidays, it doesn't change the fact that people grieve differently and for different lengths of time. No person's grief can be compared to another's.

When we return to the lodge, Adrian is still in his room. I stare at his door for a long second, willing him to be okay, before moving to the kitchen.

I make a coffee for Jordan, Evie, and me, deciding it's probably best not to disturb Adrian right now. We go for a walk. They take me to the village, where we buy muffins from a cute bakery and take them to the beach that's mostly covered in pebbles, sitting on a rusting bench to eat.

Adrian is still in his room when we get back. I check the kitchen sides for signs of life—anything to tell me he's at least eaten—and relax when I see a new plate in the sink.

"Don't worry about him," Evie tells me, noticing how my eyes move to his door. "He'll come around eventually. He always does. We just need to give him some space first."

I nod, knowing all about the need for space, and follow her into the living area.

An hour later, when we're in the middle of an intense game of *Frustration*—one I think might never end—Adrian's door opens.

I'm the only one who pauses.

He crosses the hall without looking our way, disappearing into the bathroom, and I sit straighter, hoping he's finally ready to join us. But he has his hood up when he comes into the living area, his face turned down. The pang in my chest wonders if it's because he's been crying.

"We were thinking of going out for dinner," Evie tells him without looking up from the game. "You in?"

"I'll sort myself out."

I don't miss the way Adrian's eyes never lift as he throws on his jacket and walking boots. Maybe it isn't because he's been crying. Maybe it's because of the Christmas decorations that now seem to be glaringly in our faces.

When he's out of the lodge, I turn to Evie. "Are you sure he's okay?"

"Who, Adrian?" She moves her counter three times. "He's fine. He's probably just gone to meet Molly at the pub."

"Who's Molly?" Jordan asks. His four counters are currently stuck at home until he rolls a six, and he's definitely getting frustrated.

"A girl who lives in the village. They hook up every time he's here."

I stare at the closed door as something hot flares within me. I snuff it out. "You don't think he looked... upset?"

"That's just Adrian. A moody-ass grump during the

holidays."

I want to believe her, but it's so unlike the man I saw smiling and laughing in the car.

Moving my counter between my fingers, I wonder if Evie has it wrong about her brother. If he's more affected by everything going on than she believes. After all, it can't be easy having two newcomers here at the lodge, and to top it off, a sister who demands he celebrate Christmas for them. It must make the absence of his mum glare achingly bright.

Or maybe Evie knows her brother better than I do. She's known him her entire life, and I've known him for —what? A day?

Still, I can't shake this feeling of discomfort that's settled into my bones since arriving.

*

My first morning at the lodge, I awake early. In other words, it's still dark outside my little square window, and there are no signs of life as I pad my way to the kitchen, trying to keep my steps as light as possible.

I don't switch the kettle on, even though I'm dying for a brew. Instead, I go for a glass of orange juice and hope I don't wake anyone up. Taking my glass to the double doors that lead onto the deck, I peek through the curtain, finding it pitch black outside. It isn't the kind of early morning dark that I'm used to. It's the kind that prohibits me from discerning tree from tree. Even the light from the lodge doesn't penetrate into it. It's a black sheet layering on top of another black sheet.

Shivering, I turn to face the cheery brightness of the lodge, grateful that I'm not alone in the dark out there. The Christmas decorations are what take my focus. I know what I need to do with them now. It's what I thought about all last night, way past the first rumbling sounds of Evie's snoring, and, eventually, past the sound of Adrian returning.

I'm so tired that it's all I can do not to cave and go back to bed, but this will be worth it.

This is what feels right.

I start with the easy decorations—the little gingerbread men bunting stuck to the walls, the Nutcracker figures, the garlands, the candy canes—before moving on to the wreath. I store everything in a box I find, where I assume they all came from, and try not to think about how their absence leaves the room with a little less magic. As I'm pulling down the last decoration—a star dangling from the ceiling by the window that I need to climb onto a chair to reach—I hear a door close.

I freeze.

It's still early. Early enough that I didn't anticipate anyone getting up at this time. It's not like I didn't expect them all to see what I've done eventually, but I didn't want to get caught in the act.

I brace myself, hoping for a sleepwalker, and almost fall off the chair when Adrian strolls into the room. Considering he went to bed the latest, *he* is the last one I expect to be up. He's dressed in a loose-fitted tee, and when he runs a hand through his chaotic, golden hair, the bottom lifts, revealing a toned V that disappears into his pants.

He stops still when he sees me. "Oh."

"Oh," I say in reply, eyes flicking upwards. "I thought I'd be the only one up for a while."

"I'm sorry to disappoint you."

"I'm not disappointed." Clearly, my sleepiness is making my guard slip because why else would I admit to that?

He just about smiles, and the gesture reminds me so much of the man I saw two days ago, back when it was just the two of us, and he didn't seem to hate me, that my stomach swoops.

"Why are you...?" he trails off as his eyes move upward to where my hand is still extended, ready to tear down the star. They flick around the room, taking in everything I've done, before stopping on the box packed tight with decorations. His jaw works.

"I didn't like seeing them," I blurt. Blood rushes to my

face as his eyes meet mine again. "I—er—I—" I have no idea where I'm going with this, no idea what to tell him. All I know is that I didn't think this through because what excuse am I supposed to give here? Do I tell him the truth—that I took down the decorations for him? I can't do that. "I didn't like seeing them," I repeat. "They reminded me of, um, Christmas last year, and how I always put them up with my—with my—well, I don't know. I didn't like seeing them."

Adrian's eyes scan my face so thoroughly, I'm sure he can read the lie there.

"I didn't want to tell Evie yesterday, so…"

"So you thought you'd get up early, take them down, and hope she never notices?"

"Something like it."

His lips twitch, and for one wild second, I wonder if this is why he's up so early. To take the decorations down himself.

"I think it looks better," he says, looking around the room again.

"I thought you might."

His eyes collide with mine, and I see it. An affirmation that tells me he knows why I'm really doing this.

I clear my throat. "Just this last one." I have to reach on my tiptoes to get it. The chair wobbles, making me lose balance, but before I can topple over, Adrian is somehow there, holding me steady.

I look down, finding his bright blue eyes on mine.

He doesn't look away. "We should keep at least one," he says, voice so soft it turns into shards that pierce my chest. Slowly, he moves his hand up, softly tracing his fingers against the sleeve of my jumper and stopping when he reaches my hand.

He presses down so that together, we make the star stick again.

"One is good," I say. Or, at least, I try to say it. I'm finding it a little difficult to breathe.

He lowers his hand, taking mine with it, and helps me down from the chair.

I turn my back to him. Taking a steadying breath, I return the chair to the table. All the while, I am hyperaware of his presence behind me and the unexpected effect it's having.

CHAPTER SIX

Jordan and Evie are both late risers, but when it hits nine, we deem it reasonably late enough to switch on the kettle.

I sit on the sofa while Adrian makes the brews, the sound of an early-morning breakfast show playing in the background. I'm not watching it. My thoughts are preoccupied with the man making my drink by the kitchen counter.

When Adrian sits on the adjacent sofa—the space furthest away from mine—I wonder if he's putting distance between us because of our unexpected moment earlier when he'd touched my hand. That's if he even felt anything from it. It might just be that he isn't yet comfortable enough sitting by my side, which is crazy, considering he's *slept* by my side.

Our night at the hotel couldn't seem any farther

away.

"Thanks for this," I say, hugging the mug to my chest and curling myself over its heat.

"Thanks for warning me that you're terrible at making brews," he answers.

I smirk. "I definitely did not say that just to get you to make me one."

His eyes widen. "You wouldn't. Would you?"

"I wouldn't," I confirm, but there's enough amusement in my voice to make him doubt it.

"That settles it," he throws his arm over the back of the sofa, body facing towards me. "You're brewing up next."

"I really am terrible!" I laugh.

"I'll be the judge of that." His eyes move to the TV.

As he watches the breakfast show—I still have no idea what's happening on it—I examine his side profile. No puffy eyes to suggest he's been crying, which is good, although he does seem exhausted.

I hold back a sigh. He really is a gorgeous man, and I'll curse anyone who looks this good in the morning. I swear all he needed to do to look semi-human was roll out of bed. Where's the fairness in that?

"Are you done staring at me?" he asks, eyes still on the TV.

I blink. "No."

He raises a brow, and when I glance at the TV, I see his reflection in it, staring back at me. "Are you always this unashamedly honest?" he asks.

"I wouldn't say it's without shame, but I'm definitely lacking a filter when it comes to saying things that will embarrass me. You should know that already," I add, "considering what I told you in the car."

I still can't believe I told the man sitting in front of me about my sex life—or lack thereof. But it felt right to confess at the time, and if I could go back, I'd say it again. Hearing Adrian's opinion on it has lifted some of its weight, and I'm determined to do as he said—to wait until it can be meaningful.

"Yeah. Right." He clears his throat, and if I'm not mistaken, I think those are pink blotches on his cheeks.

We drink the rest of our brews in silence. I wait for the sound that will announce Jordan and Evie are about to join us, but it doesn't come. In a strange way, I'm relieved by that.

"Should we go for a walk?" I ask when our mugs are washed and the curtains open, revealing a low mist hanging over the trees, looking frosty and mysterious and completely beautiful.

Adrian looks at me like his tiredness makes him want to protest, but he nods, and I'm springing to the hallway to get changed. By the time I'm dressed—in my multiple layers, of course—Adrian is already by the door. I pull on my trainers, using the wall for support, and notice how he's only wearing a jacket, no coat.

"It's meant to be cold out there," I say.

"I run hot, remember?"

Stuffing my hands into my coat, I follow him outside. It's so cold that I can see my breath on each exhale, puffing out like a cloud in front of me. Adrian, the madman, doesn't seem to notice.

"At least the sun is up," I say to start the conversation. "It was pitch black when I looked out the window earlier."

"We keep torches in the cupboard by the door. If you ever need to go out when it's dark, it's good to know where they are."

"Oh, no." I shake my head with vehemence. "Absolutely not. No way am I going out when it's so dark I can't see the murderer in front of me."

"To be fair, they can't see you, either."

"What if I get murdered by a herd of deer?"

He snorts. "I'd pay to see that."

"You'd pay to see a woman get murdered by a herd of deer? That's a weird kink you've got there."

"You have a weird mind."

"I know."

He smiles, and I wonder what it would take to widen

it. To get him to show teeth.

We don't really have a plan on where we're walking. It's aimless, leisurely, and I take it all in as my feet crunch on the frost beneath them. After a while, the lodges become sparse, and we reach the edge of a wood, a single dirt path trailing through it. Its only light source is from where the sun manages to break through its density.

Adrian doesn't pause before walking into it, boots crunching on fallen pine needles and broken twigs. He glances over his shoulder to check I'm following, and I step right after him.

It's so silent, I'm certain we're the only humans for miles.

It's so beautiful, I wonder why it isn't swarming with tourists.

"The park gets quiet during the winter months," Adrian explains when I voice this aloud. "Especially Christmas. Most people have families to spend it with."

My heart clenches as I think about the family who I used to spend it with. The same family who will be celebrating it now, without me. Tucking my hands deeper into my pockets, I say, "At least you have Evie. She's your family. And I'm glad I have Jordan." I take in the beauty of the tall, thin trees packed closely together, their branches entwining like they want to be as one.

Sometimes, and especially when I think about my old family, a sense of loneliness creeps up on me even when I'm in company. I try not to feel it now. "I'm glad I decided to come here."

Adrian glances sideways at me. "I'm sorry for saying I didn't want you here."

"It's okay. I get why you wouldn't."

"Answer me honestly. Did you really take those decorations down because they reminded you of your ex?"

I move my eyes to the roots threatening to trip me over. I'm a terrible, terrible liar, especially when the question is so direct, so I decide to tell the truth—or at least most of it. "It is hard," I tell him. "Spending it without him. I've sort of been dreading the day for months, just like I dreaded missing his birthday. To wake up next to the same person for seven years just to…not?" I shake my head. "I've never really felt alone before, but I guess this year I'm starting to fear it. Mum and Dad have decided to make their cruise annual, and my sister has her husband and kids."

"You have Jordan," Adrian reminds me.

"I have Jordan," I smile. "But he also has Evie now. What happens when they both decide to spend it together? When—" I cut off when I realise what I'm saying. That I'm voicing fears I swear didn't exist moments ago. Selfish fears. I should be happy that my brother has found someone, not fearing the day he decides to leave me behind.

But the look on Adrian's face tells me he understands exactly what I'm feeling, and the lack of judgement comforts me.

Adrian no longer has his mum to spend Christmas with, and seeing Evie with a partner must be double hard for him, although I'm sure he'll never admit it.

I have the sudden urge to pull him into a tight, fierce hug.

"If anyone can survive the holiday season alone," Adrian says, holding a low-hanging branch up for me to walk beneath, "it's you."

"What makes you say that?"

He steps beneath the branch after me. "You just seem…Strong."

I open my mouth and close it, realising that I have no words to say back to that. Even if I did, I don't think I'd be able to get them past the gratitude rushing through my chest. "Thank you," I manage to say. "You seem strong to me, too." So strong. This is a man who not only lost his only parental figure but who, at the first opportunity, took legal guardianship over his little sister. He comes to this place every year to honour his mum, even though it clearly opens up old wounds to do so. Would *I* be able to do that?

I hear the splash of Adrian's foot stomping into water, and I stop still at the sight before me.

There is a huge, sloshing puddle before us, basically a swamp, that covers the pathway for a good number of yards. By the base of the trees on either side, there's mud so thick that I swear I'd lose both shoes in it.

"What's the matter?" Adrian asks, turning to see why I've stopped.

"Shouldn't we...turn around?"

"Why would we do that?" Ignoring the swamp like it isn't a major drawback, Adrian steps further into it, the murky water covering the toes of his waterproof boots—smart of him to bring them—and slushing up his ankles. He turns, waiting for me to join him, which I'd gladly let him wait a long time for.

"I have a bit of a shoe problem," I admit.

"What?" He looks down with a frown, shaking his head at what he finds—my trainers, very much not waterproof and likely to soak the whole swamp up. "You have *got* to be kidding me."

"I'm sorry." I look around, trying to find another way to get past the sludge and water, but the frost seems to have evaded this patch.

"So you're telling me," Adrian continues, stepping towards me, "that you thought to bring a blanket—no, wait, that you thought to bring *this*," —he pulls on the tassel of my hoodie—"and *this*," —the cuff of my winter coat—"and *this*," —he tugs on the bauble of my hat—"but not waterproof boots?"

"Shoes are always the last thing I think about."

"Clearly." At least he looks amused. "Do you at least have some at the lodge if we go back for them?" The look on my face must give him the answer. "Oh, Ophelia. Ophelia, Ophelia, Ophelia." He drops his head into his hand before lifting it. "I really can't take you anywhere, can I?"

"Hey, it's not my fault nobody gave me the shoe memo."

"I'll let Evie know that your common sense is lacking." I fold my arms as he continues to taunt, "That way if we go somewhere tropical next time, she can remind you to bring a hat." Reaching my arm out, I try to swat him, but he steps back. "If you want to get violent, you'll have to step in here."

"There is no way I'm stepping into that. I have my shoes to think about."

"Oh, so now you think about them?" I walked into that one. Adrian flashes me a grin—the one I wanted to see—and in one quick movement, he steps forward, pulls on the tassel of my hoodie, and steps back again.

"Don't make me come in there," I warn.

He flashes me another grin, and my heart pinches at the sight of it, playful and devilish and oh-so rare.

Then he does something that I don't expect.

He crouches in front of me, back facing my direction.

"What are you doing?" I ask. Surely, he doesn't mean what I think he means.

"Coming up with a solution. If you can't walk through it, I'll carry you through it. It'll be a shame if you miss the view at the end of here because of your poor choice of shoes."

"Alright." I teeter where I'm stood, afraid I'll either hurt him in my attempts to climb on or fall face forward into the swamp. Worst still, what if Adrian decides to toss me into the water as punishment for my choice of shoes?

"I've got you," he says, noticing my hesitation.

I nod, and in a leap of faith, I jump, catching onto his shoulders and clinging with all my might.

My worry is unnecessary. Adrian catches me with ease, hoisting me upright without so much as a grunt. "You weigh less than my bag," he says, curling his hands around my thighs.

"I can't tell if that's supposed to be an insult."

"Just an observation." His hands tighten around my legs—another thing that feels too intimate, too close.

It's just a piggyback, I tell myself. *That's all Adrian*

thinks of it.

As he wades us through the water, I observe the top of his head, mesmerised by the thickness of his hair. The waves remind me of licks of flames curling towards the sun in shades of honey and caramel and copper. He's a golden cockapoo in human form.

"Can I ask you something?" he says.

"Go ahead."

"Evie told you about our mum, didn't she?"

I open my mouth before second-guessing myself. This is a sensitive subject, and I don't want to accidentally say something insensitive through my lack of thinking.

"She did tell me," I answer. "But she didn't share anything overly personal, and if you don't want to talk about it, you don't need to."

He nods, the top of his shaggy hair bobbing. "I just want to know one thing."

"Alright."

"Is learning about my mum the real reason you took the decorations down?" After a second, he adds, "I know you said it was because of your ex, but I don't buy it. You would have kept them up if this was about you."

I take a shaky breath, surprised that he thinks so well of me. Then again, why shouldn't he know the truth? If admitting the truth means he knows he has someone on his side, however distant the two of us may be, isn't that a good thing? And isn't it one of my mantras to never hide the truth from someone just because I don't know how they'll take it?

"Yes," I answer. "That is the reason."

His hands loosen around my thighs before tightening again. "Why? Because you felt sorry for me?"

"Because I didn't think it was fair for Evie not to warn you. And I felt bad about what I said to you at the pub. My assumptions were way off."

"You thought an ex-girlfriend broke my heart," he remembers with a scoff. "Like any girl could break my heart after—" He cuts off, but I hear the rest of the sentence without him needing to finish it. *After it broke from losing my mum.*

My heart throbs.

"Now I want you to know one thing," I say, looking down at him.

He tenses beneath me. "Go on."

"If at any point it gets too much for you this week, if there's a crappy Christmas song on that you want turning off or a decoration you want burning, you can come to me, and I'll do the deed for you." I already feel better for saying it. Better for being here. If I hadn't said yes to Evie when she'd asked, it would just be her, Jordan, and Adrian, and the latter would still be a stranger.

It's several beats before he says anything. When he does, it's through a clog of emotion. "Thank you, Ophelia. That means...a lot."

He stops walking. It's only then that I realise we're no longer in swamp territory and haven't been for a while.

"Ready for me to lower you?" he asks.

"You can carry me for longer if you want."

His chuckle drifts up to me, and to my surprise, he actually continues walking. "Don't think I won't be charging you for this," he says, peering back to look at me. "My services don't come free." He moves his hands up my thigh, hoisting me higher as he adjusts his grip.

"You should always agree to a price before you deliver the service," I say, feeling heat wherever his fingers move. "Didn't anybody ever teach you that?"

We reach the end of the trail. It curves to the left from here, continuing its route back from where we came. Ahead of us, the trees thin, and there's a beaten wooden fence separating the woodland from the fields beyond. Adrian lowers me when we reach it.

I would thank him for the ride, but I'm too busy ogling at the view before me. So much openness. So much frosted grass glistening beneath the rising sun and so many blues in a sky that stretches for miles uninterrupted.

"Told you it'd be a shame if you missed this," Adrian says, stepping beside me. He leans his hands against the fence, eyes meeting mine—eyes that are the exact shade as where the pale blue sky starts to deepen.

I remember to exhale. "You were right."

He looks out at the fields with a sigh that I feel in my bones. "I sometimes forget how beautiful it is here."

My eyes stay locked on his face. "Because you miss your mum?"

He inhales deeply, his tendons visible as he grips the fence. "Yes." His voice is soft, almost resigned. He peers down at me. "Can I ask you something?"

"You can ask me anything." I mean that. Whether I can give him an answer is something we'll figure out.

Looking back at the fields, a frown permeates his features. "Do you think I'm wrong for not wanting to celebrate Christmas?"

As the question sinks into me, I give myself time to unravel my answer. I could tell him what I know he wants to hear, but that's just another way of hiding the truth and choosing what's easy.

Turning to face the view with him, I place my hands beside his on the fence. "I think Evie's right. I think your mum would want you to celebrate Christmas. I think she would want you to enjoy it like you would have had she still been here. But that doesn't make you wrong." I turn to face him, finding him watching me with nervous eyes, braced like he's held together only by a taut string. "Just because it's what your mum would have wanted doesn't mean it's what you should want. And I know that might sound wrong. I don't mean it to sound disrespectful—"

"—It doesn't sound disrespectful—"

"—But it's easier said than done, isn't it? Moving on. It's what your mum would have wanted for you, so you should do it. But when you're the one who's left behind —when you're the one who aches in their absence—" I stop and shake my head, turning to face the fields again. "You're not wrong for not wanting to celebrate Christmas, Adrian. Definitely not."

He's silent for so long that I feel incapable of speaking into it. Glancing at him, I find him with his head lowered, shoulders sagged.

"Are you alright?" I ask, sudden worry making me dip my head to get a better look at him.

It startles me to hear him laugh. "I'm alright." He stands straighter, turning to face me with a smile. "I feel as though a weight has been lifted from me. Like...I'm understood."

Heat blooms on my cheeks, but it's nothing compared to the warmth rushing through me.

Understood. How long have we both felt the

opposite?

*

When we return to the lodge, Jordan and Evie are finally up. I can see them through the glass door as we make our way towards it. I can also see how Adrian steps away from me like he's purposefully trying to regain his distance.

Evie's face is a rare storm when we enter. I glance at Adrian, seeing as the glare is aimed at him, wondering what he might have done to upset her.

"You couldn't have left the decorations up for one day for us, could you?" *Oh, crap.* "*One day,*" she continues to seethe. "I told you Ophelia was finding it tough this year. I told you she needed cheering up. I even told you that Jordan didn't want to come here unless we had *something* Christmas related. And you do this? How *could* you?"

"I'm sorry." My eyes dart to Adrian, hardly believing he's willing to take the fall for this when it's all on me.

"No." I take a step towards Evie, wishing I'd thought more about the repercussions when I'd taken the decorations down. I'd only thought of Adrian. "It was me," I say, stomach twisting at the admission. "I was the one who took them down."

Slowly, Evie's eyes move to me, confusion replacing their anger. "What?"

I take a deep breath.

"Ophelia, you don't need to do this," Adrian says from behind me.

"I took them down," I repeat, glancing at him in time to see his eyes soften. "I'm sorry. I just...I thought I could do this. That I'd be okay. But everything is different this year, everything is...It's..." I think about that first Christmas when Adrian and Evie came back here without their mum, how it must have felt. I think about the family I was a part of for several years and how I'm now just...not.

I think about how some people come into your life, and despite your deepest desires to have them stay, they leave, taking the back exit and locking the door behind them.

"Oh, Ophelia." Evie rushes forward, pulling me into a hug I don't deserve. "It's alright. We don't need them up. I'm so sorry."

"No, no. Please don't be sorry, Evie. This isn't your fault."

She brushes away my tears—tears I hadn't been aware were there. "Let me get you a tissue."

She comes back with a full roll.

I feel utterly ridiculous as I dab at my eyes.

Adrian stares at me like he doesn't know what to do.

"Me and Jord were going to go out for a late

breakfast," she tells me. "Do you want to join us?"

"No. You two should go together. I'll be fine. I'm just," I wave my tissue in the air, "having an unexpected moment."

She leaves to get changed, but only after making sure I have no tears left.

I couldn't have asked for anyone better for Jordan.

When she's gone, Jordan turns to face me. "I'm sorry, Phi. I know you still get upset over him. But after what Evie told us about wanting to celebrate Christmas this year?" He frowns. "This was selfish of you." He leaves, too, following Evie into their bedroom.

A wave of sadness crashes into me. In a way, I was being selfish—I hadn't thought about Evie when I'd taken the decorations down. I'd thought only of Adrian and of the crying, wounded boy who still grieved for his mother.

I feel a squeeze on my shoulder and look up to find Adrian peering down at me, his eyes a softer wave, the kind you can't help but relax into. "Thank you," he says gently. "I mean it."

It almost makes it worth it.

CHAPTER SEVEN

Adrian

I toss and turn beneath the covers.

I haven't been able to sleep, a fact that might put me in a bad mood if I weren't feeling foul already.

Those damned decorations. Why did Evie need to put them up without warning me? Better yet, why did Ophelia need to take them down?

Why does this need to be so fucking difficult?

Swinging my feet from the bed, I drop my head into my hands.

Mum, if you're out there, I'd appreciate it if you could give me the answers.

Stupid thought. Wherever my mum is, I'm sure it isn't anywhere near here. And who am I kidding, anyway? I already know the answer.

Quietly, I open my door and creep into the hallway. The living area is exactly as we'd left it last night—bare. Zero festivity, and not a hint to suggest it's Christmas. Well, that's unless you count the star dangling by the window, the one I told Ophelia we should keep up in a moment of clear madness.

I remember the feel of her small hand beneath mine and rapidly shove the thought away. I should have just left it there, but no, I had to offer to carry her during our morning walk in another moment of madness, so now I have the feel of her clinging to my back as another memory I need to shove far down.

Looking around the room, I spot the box stuffed with Christmas decorations beneath the table. I'd really rather not feel guilty on top of everything else I feel at this time of the year, but here I am, about a second away from voting myself as the worst human. Because out of the four people staying beneath this roof, I'm the only one who doesn't want the decorations up, and thanks to the heart of a girl who barely knows me, I've gotten my way.

When Jordan called Ophelia selfish, I felt a knife twist in my gut. She may be the one to have taken the decorations down, but she did this for me, not herself, and I'm the only one who knows it.

Jordan was right about one thing, though. Taking the

decorations down *has* upset Evie. My sister wants to celebrate Christmas, and, thanks to me, she hasn't been able to. How long have I gotten my way? There's a voice at the back of my brain, one I'd rather ignore, telling me that it's been for far too long.

With a sigh, I pull the box out from beneath the table.

It feels...*wrong* celebrating Christmas without Mum here to celebrate it with. To me, it's like sending a message that reads, *We can do this without you. We can enjoy this without you.* But it feels...wrong to my core upsetting Evie like this. Evie: a girl I would literally die for.

And it isn't just us this year, as she's so rightly pointed out. We have Jordan and Ophelia here, too. And while Ophelia seemed genuinely upset when she talked about her ex-boyfriend earlier, I also know that she wants—*needs*—these decorations up as much as Evie. I didn't miss how her face became alight when she walked into the lodge for the first time. She had the same reaction when we entered the hotel and that stupid festive pub we'll probably never speak about again.

I pull a nutcracker from the box with another sigh. "This is for you, Evie." *And I guess it's for you, too*, I add, glancing at the hanging star.

I must admit, once I'm finished hanging the decorations up—trying my best to do a half-decent job

—the room looks nothing like it did when Evie was in charge. It wasn't a joyous or merry or magical experience for me, either, like I'm sure it was for her. Still, they're up, the lodge is festive again, and everyone is still sleeping.

I head back to my room, pausing outside my door. My eyes move to the room at the end of the hallway as I question whether or not I should warn Ophelia about what I've done. If she wakes up and shows complete surprise at the decorations being there, we aren't going to pull this off as her being the one who did it.

I walk to her door, raising my hand and pausing again. What exactly do I tell her? *Hey, it's me, I've put the decorations back up. Want to take claim for it?* And what if she's asleep? *Of course she's still asleep, idiot, it's five in the morning.* Maybe I should come back later. Or I could just disappear for the day and let them believe Santa himself put them up.

"Are you trying to scare me?" The whisper comes from the other side of the door. My head jolts upright, but I'm too off guard to respond. "I can hear you out there," Ophelia continues in that shaky whisper. "Say something comforting before I'm paralysed by fear."

"It's me."

A beat. "Adrian?"

That shouldn't excite me as much as it does. "Yeah.

Still scared?"

"That depends. Are you possessed by an evil spirit come to claim my soul?"

My lips pull up. What an imagination. "If I were, I wouldn't tell you that now, would I?"

"How comforting." The door creaks open. Through the slit, I see Ophelia's single hazel eye peeping through, darkened by the night around her. "You don't look possessed," she whispers.

"Don't be fooled," I whisper back. "I might be biding my time."

The door widens. Ophelia flicks her light on, and my eyes scroll down, stopping on her exposed thighs stretching beneath the hem of her fluffy grey nightdress.

It shouldn't be sexy, but it is.

"So are you outside my room for a reason?" she asks as I flick my eyes to hers. "Or is it just to scare me? Because I should warn you, ghosts don't scare me half as much as they used to. I'm more afraid of the living."

I try not to smile, but that already seems like a very Ophelia thing to say. "I have something to show you." I nod to the end of the hallway and turn, feeling a thrill when she follows me out.

"What is it?"

Glancing over my shoulder, I find her right behind

me, peeking around my arm like she's ready to use me as a shield if something unfavourable jumps out. Little does she know I'm willing to be that shield without her asking. I open the door to the living area and her ensuing gasp has me suddenly wanting to hide.

"The decorations are up." She says it like it's something she can't believe.

"Yeah." I clear my throat. "They are."

Her eyes dart to mine. "You did this."

"Yeah," I say again, trying not to look away from her. "I did."

She steps further inside. "This is—I—You—" Gingerly, she touches the wreath on the fireplace, her small hands half its size, before turning to face me again. "Adrian."

Heat rises up my face at the tenderness in her voice. "It's not…that big of a deal."

"Not that big of a deal?" She takes a step towards me before second-guessing herself. I'm torn between wanting to close the gap and wanting to regain it. "This is…You didn't want them up." Her eyes are filled with so much emotion that I can feel my throat clogging. "You didn't need to do this. Really. Why did you?"

"It didn't feel fair that everyone else was suffering because of me."

Her eyes scan my face. She has this remarkable way of making you feel like she's reading things about you that you don't know yourself. "You didn't make anyone suffer."

"Come on. We both know I did."

She watches me for a few seconds longer. "It still doesn't mean that you needed to do this."

"I didn't *want* to do this," I admit. "Believe me. It still feels…wrong. But at least this way, Evie can get the Christmas she wants, and you can be vindicated from this terrible deed you did." I intend for the last part to make her smile, but instead, she seems to be on the verge of tears, eyes watering until the brink of pooling out.

Shit.

"Unless you don't want them up," I quickly add, worried that they do in fact remind her of her ex, and by putting them back up, I've done the last thing she needs. "If they upset you—"

"No." She shakes her head. "I'm not upset. This," she wipes at a tear with a soft laugh. "This is because I'm proud. I think what you've done here is brave. I know it wasn't easy and that it must cause you pain. Not many people would choose that. So—thank you. I really wanted them up."

My mouth works.

I'm…speechless.

This woman has robbed me of my ability to not only

use words but also to find them.

"So did you get me out of bed early to show me this?" Ophelia asks. "Or is there something else?"

"No, it was this." I clear my throat. "I thought you should see it before the other two get up. It'll be weird if they think I did this considering the reason they think *you* took them down."

"Good thinking." She smiles before turning back to the decorations. "They might think you did it out of spite because you hate me."

"I mean, they wouldn't be wrong..." I smirk at the look she gives me. When she realises I'm joking, she laughs, the sound igniting a fire in my chest.

"I should probably redo them, though. Evie would never believe I did this. No offense."

Now it's my turn to laugh. "None taken. I thought it myself."

"It's a good job you got me up early." She rolls her sleeves up as she looks at the tinsel hanging lopsided on the TV stand. "This is going to take hours to fix."

"Smart ass."

I do my best to help her, but, in the end, I'm more of a hindrance, so I stand nearby as help on hand. Twice, she needs my assistance steadying the chair so she can stand on it. I do it, but it isn't without regret that she's wearing a dress. Each time she reaches, it rises, showing more of her thigh, and even though I don't look, my imagination isn't so polite.

For crying out loud, the girl is wearing reindeer socks. Why is my heart beating like it's attracted to her?

"Just this last one," she says, reaching on her tiptoes. *Keep your eyes on her face.* "Okay." She searches blindly for something. It takes me a second to realise she's wanting my hand. I take both of hers and help her down, stepping away the second her feet touch the floor.

She looks around the room, taking in the improved décor.

"I liked it better when I did it," I say from her side.

She nudges my ribs. "Smart ass."

Fuck. Me. Why do I want to sweep her into my arms and have her do exactly that?

With the decorations done, I leave her, needing the safety of my bedroom walls. I sprawl out on my bed and run a hand down my face, well aware that I need to relieve myself, but when I close my eyes, it's Ophelia I see, and I refuse to jerk off to her. Not when it can never happen for real.

She wants meaningful. Sex with me can never be that.

And I...don't want to be the one she regrets.

*

The smell of bacon drifts down the hall when I awake

from an uneasy sleep. I finally feel ready to face Ophelia again, even if she did manage to make her way into my dreams.

"We're making a full English," Jordan tells me as I make my way into the living area. He's standing by the hob with Evie by his side. Considering the size of the kitchen, they're shoulder-to-shoulder. "Do you want in?"

"Sure." I lean my arms against the counter, my eyes sweeping to Ophelia before darting back again. "Do you need a hand?"

"Nope. We've got this. Thanks."

"No problem." I drum my fingers against the counter. It doesn't take long for me to notice the way my sister is looking at me. It's like she's waiting for me to explode. "What's the matter?" I ask.

"Don't get mad." She turns, arm brushing against Jordan thanks to the tiny space, and holds out her hands. "But...Ophelia has put the decorations back up." She scrunches her eyes closed as she waits for the impact. I hold back a smile.

"Oh. Yeah," I say, feigning surprise.

Her eyes pop open again. "You're alright with it? And Ophelia—you're sure you're okay with this, too?"

"I'm positive." Ophelia, thankfully, is now in jeans. No thigh exposure. "I really, really want to celebrate

Christmas with you all. Yesterday was just a glitch."

"I want to celebrate it, too," I say. It feels like pushing against a solid boulder getting the words out, but when Evie's eyes widen at my declaration, I manage a smile.

"Holy mother of Christmas." She barrels towards me, knocking Jordan to the side in her haste, and wraps her arms around my neck. "Thank you, thank you, thank you," she says with three kisses on my cheek.

"I'll *try* to celebrate it," I amend, pulling away. "I can't promise I'll be festive from morning until night."

"That's good enough for me." She gives me a squeeze before stepping back, eyes so bright and beaming that I regret not trying this for her sooner.

"Who's making the brews?" Jordan asks as he sweeps bacon onto each of our plates.

My lips curve upward as I look over at Ophelia and remember the promise she made me yesterday. "Ophelia is."

"Phi?" Jordan's head shoots up like I've just told him a six-year-old will be making his morning coffee. "Nah. That would be a mistake. She makes shit brews."

"I told you," Ophelia says.

My brow quirks at the triumph in her voice. "And I told you that I'll be the judge of it."

"It's your regret." Shrugging, she moves past me, manoeuvring her way to the kettle.

When I realise I'm still watching her, I quickly join Jordan, helping him carry the plates over to the table before taking the seat opposite Evie.

Ophelia drops a mug in front of me before taking the free seat at my side. "Judge away," she says, planting her chin in her hand as she waits for my verdict.

I sip slowly, cautiously, aware that I now have every eye at the table aimed my way. Once I've tasted a few sips, I smack my lips together and conclude, "This truly is the shittest brew I've ever tasted."

Everyone laughs, Ophelia included.

"I *told* you I'm bad at making them." Her eyes dance in delight. "I hope this serves as a lesson." It's her glee that makes me do it. She should lose at least *some* face at making the worst brew I've ever tasted. "What are you doing?" she asks as I push out my chair.

"The only person getting served a lesson this morning is you. Come on. I'll show you how it's done."

She follows me to the kitchen. It's just like this morning all over again, with a thrill shooting through me at seeing her join me.

"You aren't supposed to be enjoying this, you know," I say as I drop a teabag into each mug.

She stands on her tiptoes. "I'm getting taught how to make a brew by Adrian Wilde. How can I not be excited?"

My stomach flips at her use of my full name. But of course she knows it. She knows it because of Evie. "Well then," I force calmness into my voice, "you better listen carefully, Ophelia Jones, because this is a once-in-a-lifetime lesson."

After I show her how to do it right—brew it, squeeze it, add milk at the end—we finish eating and go our separate ways to get ready.

At lunch, we all decide to head into the village to show Ophelia the local pub.

"Hey, you." Evie falls back to walk beside me. "How's it going?"

"Alright." I stuff my hands into the front pocket of my hoodie, eyes on Ophelia wearing those damned trainers. "You?"

"It's going alright for me, too." She looks ahead. I think that's all she has to say before she clears her throat. "I have something to say to you, but I hope you don't take it the wrong way."

"I'll try my best not to."

"Ophelia is off-limits."

My eyes dart to her face. "What? I already know that."

"Okay. Alright." She raises her hands. "I just wanted to make extra sure that you know not to make a move on her."

I love my sister, but sometimes she can annoy the hell

out of me. "As I already said, I know not to make a move on her." It doesn't matter how much I want to. Or how much it surprises me that I want to. We're here for a week—I can resist her for that long.

"Good. Because the last thing Ophelia needs is to be somebody's one-night-only." I turn my face away, but it doesn't stop her from continuing. "I'm sorry if it sounds like I'm being mean, but I'm serious. She doesn't deserve it."

"I know she doesn't deserve it." God, after spending a single day with her, I figured that one out.

I can feel Evie's eyes on me, but I stare resolutely away from her.

"She's a special girl," she says.

"She is." Shit. I did *not* mean to say that out loud. "But it doesn't mean that I want to make a move," I quickly add. "I don't."

"Sure thing. Just make sure you stay away from her." She walks ahead, skipping the last few steps as she catches up with Ophelia and loops their arms together.

I feel a stab of envy that I quickly dismiss. I haven't even done anything yet, and I'm being told to stay away. How is it even possible when we're sharing the same lodge? What am I supposed to do—only come out of my room when Ophelia goes into hers?

When we enter the pub, I hear somebody call my

name. Molly. She waves at me from the corner where she's sitting with her aunt, uncle, and cousin, whose names I can never remember, all dressed in their disgusting Christmas jumpers. I wave back, but I refrain from going over. I already had a drink with her two days ago, and spending too much time with one girl is something I try avoid.

"Remember what I said yesterday?" Ophelia says, appearing by my side.

Speaking of spending too much time with one girl. "Which part exactly?"

"That if it gets too much for you, you can tell me?" Her eyes are ahead as she speaks, her voice quiet in a way that makes me feel like a conspirator. "If you want the Christmas music off, I'm not opposed to throwing water on the jukebox."

I almost choke on a laugh. "Why don't you just unplug it? Or do you prefer destroying things?"

"Destroying things, definitely." She gives me a sly smile as she walks ahead, giving me the sudden urge to see her destroy me.

Thanks to Evie and Jordan sitting beside one another, I again find myself by Ophelia's side. The tight space means we're pushed together, arms and thighs touching. I wish I could say that I'm not affected by it, but I'm acutely aware of every part of me connected to her. It's like she's whirring those nerve endings to life and shutting down everywhere else. Well, not everywhere. There's one part of me that seems incapable of sleeping whenever she's around.

"I think I'm in the mood for a bottle of wine," Evie says, eyes scanning the menu. "You like white, don't you, Ophelia?"

"I do. And I will definitely halve that with you."

As we wait for our drinks to be brought over, Molly makes an appearance, her cousin—*damn it, what's his name?*—in tow.

"Hey, guys," she says, her eyes lingering a second too long on Ophelia before brightening upon seeing my sister. "Evie! It's been too long."

"Oh, hey, Molly!" Evie stands, wrapping her arms around Molly in that too-friendly way of hers. "How've you been?"

"I've been really good, actually. I'm playing Snow White in this year's pantomime."

"That's amazing! I remember you playing a tree when we were, like, ten."

Molly laughs. "From a tree to Snow White. I've really progressed."

"This is my boyfriend, Jordan, by the way," Evie says, turning to make introductions. "And his sister, Ophelia. And you already know Adrian, of course."

"Of course." Molly's smile widens when she looks at me. "Do you remember my cousin, Eric?"

"Yeah. Eric." So that's his name. "Yeah, I remember him."

He nods at me before moving his eyes to my right. My muscles tense when I realise his obvious fixation on Ophelia.

"We came to ask if you guys are coming to the Christmas Eve Eve party in two days," Molly says. I try to keep my attention on her, but it's difficult when I can feel Ophelia's leg against my own, moving as she gets closer.

"What's got you so tense?" she whispers into my ear, making my body react in a way that it shouldn't. "Is it the Christmas jumpers? Because I'm not averse to throwing a jug of gravy on them."

I cover my mouth to stop a laugh from coming out.

Fuck it if she isn't going to be the death of me.

"Christmas Eve Eve?" Jordan is now asking. "Why not a Christmas Eve party?"

"We're sort of a family village," Molly answers. "We party on Christmas Eve Eve and spend the next day with family. It'll be good if the two of you finally come to one," she adds, looking from Evie to me.

"We'll be there," Evie confirms for all of us. I quirk a brow at her, but she just throws me a shrug in response. "If we've decided to celebrate, we may as well go all out, right?"

After we finish drinking, we order food, and when our plates are cleared, I make the rash decision to stay behind while the others head back to the lodge. My logic: given my current reactions towards Ophelia, it's best if I do stay away from her, and while I'd rather not spend more time with Molly, she feels less of a risk than the girl whose leg I can still feel against my own.

Sounds like a solid plan, except when I creep into the lodge beneath the light of the moon, Ophelia is the only one there.

"Evie got a taste for the wine," she explains as I edge into the room. "Her and Jordan are at the onsite bar."

She has her feet tucked onto the sofa, a blanket draped over her legs, and as I try to move to the hallway, out of her way, she taps the space by her side. "Come join me. I've been alone for hours, and your company isn't so bad."

"Alright." Lowing myself into the space beside her, I try to not squirm at our close proximity—or the fact that we're here alone.

"What're you watching?" I ask.

"Love Actually. It's my favourite Christmas movie." She seems happy until her eyes suddenly widen. "Crap. I'm so sorry. Let me turn this off—"

She reaches for the remote. I must be going crazy

because I reach for it with her, my hand layering on top of hers to stop her from switching it over. "It's fine. I don't mind."

She stares at me. "You—you're sure? I'm guessing Christmas movies aren't your favourite, either?"

"It's fine," I say again, quickly pulling my hand away. It's a few seconds before she lowers hers. "I'm curious to see what makes it your favourite."

"It's because it has everything." Tucking the remote away, she looks back at the TV with a quiet smile. "The good, the bad, the beautiful, the ugly. Every side that love has to offer. And who doesn't want to watch the Prime Minister fall for someone who says shit, fuck, and piss-it all in the same meeting?"

"That happens?" I look at the screen with new intrigue, but in the end, it's Ophelia holding my attention.

Her face is so expressive. One moment, she's laughing, and the next, she's looking so sad, like her heart is breaking for these fictional characters who don't exist. And then she's sighing like she's watching the sweetest thing she's ever seen.

I stare at her for a long time. Finally, when I can't hold it in any longer, I whisper, "How do you do it?"

She pulls her eyes from the screen. "Do what?"

I think about how I can barely stand to be in a room

with Christmas decorations, and here she is, voluntarily watching a movie about people falling in and out of love. "How do you watch a romance? How do you —" I nod at the screen as Colin Firth's character asks for the daughter's hand in marriage. "Watch *this* after everything that's happened to you?" *How do you keep your heart from shattering so all you're left with are these broken pieces you're afraid will keep breaking?*

Ophelia frowns as she considers. I realise I like it when she does that. Contemplates her words before giving them. "It isn't...without pain," she begins. "Whenever I see a proposal or two people confessing their forever love to one another, I have this moment where my heart just stops like it doesn't want to feel anymore. I remember the time when I thought I had that kind of love, and when I think about how it ended, I'm paralysed with this grief that I can't quite explain.

"But," her eyes soften as she looks back at the screen. "I love love. I love being in love, giving love, and being a human capable of experiencing it. I was a sucker for romance before I met him, I was a sucker for romance while I was with him, and I'll be a sucker for romance until the day I die. That's *my* thing. No one can take it away from me." She tucks her knees higher, propping her chin on them. "After the break-up, my mum told me I love too much. But how can anybody love *too much?* I love how you're supposed to love. Intensely. Passionately. Unconditionally. Sometimes quietly. I love with the promise of forever, and while it hurts to be left by someone who doesn't feel the same, I wouldn't want to be different. Wearing my heart on my sleeve is better than keeping it locked away."

She falls silent.

The movie continues.

I can't look away from her.

This...This is what I won't be able to resist. Not the physical attraction. That I can handle. It's...her. Her mind. Her thoughts. The way she talks about love even after being wounded by it. The way her smile seems to hold a thousand secrets.

She makes me want to know what it is to be loved by her.

She makes me want to feel what it is to be in love.

My heart is beating erratically. I look at the TV, hoping to calm it—hoping, too, that it's the alcohol marring my thoughts—when she speaks again.

"Do you want to know what the worst part is? The part of the break-up that nobody tells you about?"

I look back at her, enraptured. "What is it?"

"It's the loss of everyone else. The mum and dad you loved. The sister and brother you saw as family. The aunts, the gran—all the people you thought you'd be a part of forever. They just...disappear. And then you start to wonder if you were nothing to begin with. If you were always an extension of him, never a standalone, and now that he's cut you off, you're..."

"Nothing."

"Nothing," she repeats. "And then there's the friends." She wipes at her nose, new tears forming. "Over the years, I've witnessed enough breakups to know that it's the girlfriend who disappears. I never thought it would happen to me, but I've become non-existent to them. The messages, they just...stopped. The group chats continued without me. And the one time I did see them all out, there was this pause like they were holding their breath and bracing themselves for something. Bracing themselves for me. I was no longer human to them. I was the Dreaded Ex-Girlfriend." She wraps her arms around her knees, hugging them as if it's what's holding her together. "That's why I stopped going out. I couldn't bear to be looked at like that when all I did was love someone."

Somewhere between her starting to speak and finishing, I've edged closer. She doesn't say anything else, and since I have no words to comfort her, I wrap my arm around her shoulder and draw her in.

She rests her cheek on my shoulder.

We're wordless after that, watching the movie in

silence, never moving from that position.

We stay like that for a long time after.

CHAPTER EIGHT

On either side of me, niche, independent stores line the cobbled streets, looking like they've been plucked straight out of a Christmas storybook. Outdoor Christmas lights hang from left to right, and a ginormous Christmas tree pierces the sky in the town square, gleaming red and green, with a star that's bigger than my head on top.

It was a good idea of Evie's to come here in the late afternoon, just as the sky is morphing from a frosty blue to a deeper, inkier shade. Stars twinkle over our heads, and in the distance, the last of the sun can be seen setting over the sea.

"This place is magical," I say again.

Evie smiles from over her shoulder. "If you think this is magical, wait until you see in here."

I follow her inside a store, the door giving a pleasant

ding as it opens. As soon as we're inside, my senses are hit with a smell so heavenly—think cinnamon and candy and roasted apples—I have to inhale deeper.

"Okay," I say. "I vote we spend the rest of the day in here."

She laughs. "I come in here every year. A girl can never have too many candles."

The candles line every wall, but they aren't your average kind—these ones have a bit of magic sprinkled into each one. Some hold crystals inside—rubies, sapphires, onyx's—while others have rose petals or dried buds or little sprigs of rosemary sprinkled on top.

Holding a vanilla-scented one to my nose, I peek over my shoulder at the door, but Adrian and Jordan haven't followed us inside.

That's been the case this entire trip. Adrian, for whatever reason, hasn't said a single word to me.

I swear the man has many facets. No one from the outside would believe that just last night, Adrian had comforted me while I'd had *another* one of my unexpected emotional confessions. I say 'unexpected' like this hasn't been my life this past year. At any given moment, I can go from being the happiest in the room to the saddest with no idea what made me switch. Although it sucks, I know it's part of the healing process, so all I can do is walk through it and resist the urge to run.

And Adrian is surprisingly easy to open up to.

Maybe this is why he isn't speaking to me today. Maybe I've drained him, emotionally speaking, and this is his way of telling me he doesn't want to hear any more on the subject. I can't blame him for that. Everyone has a tolerance level when it comes to emotional baggage, and if this is him putting boundaries in place, I should respect them.

"What about this one?" Evie asks, holding up a candle from one of the display tables.

I walk over, sticking my nose inside. It smells of pine needles and apples with a hint of spiced wine. *Winter by the Fire*, I read from the label.

"It's perfect for you," I say.

She ends up buying three more. I go away with two —*Enchanted Library* because I really couldn't resist, and *Lost Books Waiting to be Found* because how could I not buy a candle with that name?

Outside, the sun has completely set. Our breaths puff out into misty clouds, and a thin sheet of ice threatens to upturn us if we aren't careful where we walk.

I take slow, careful steps, eyes on the ground so that by the time I follow Evie inside another store, I have no idea what I've just walked into.

"I knew we'd find you in here."

I look up, eyes colliding with Adrian's as he stands

by a display cabinet in the middle of the store. He looks swiftly away, so I do, too, examining instead the uniqueness of the place. It looks ready to burst, with so many random objects that I have no idea what to look at first—the swords on the wall, the rows of colourful comic books, the miniature figurines or the movie replicas. Clearly, it's a store for collectors. It's also, without a doubt, the coolest store I've ever been inside.

I can't help but voice my awe as I walk around. "This is the coolest thing I've ever seen," I say. "No, *this* is the coolest thing I've ever seen. No, wait *this* is!"

"Phi," Jordan calls over to me. "I love you, but you're annoying the hell out of me."

"Sorry." I drop the mushroom-shaped crystal I'd been holding and look up when I hear a snigger.

Adrian is a row in front of me, browsing through a stack of comic books with a smirk ticking up one side of his lips. If I didn't know any better, I'd think he was laughing at me. But he can't be doing that. He isn't paying enough attention to me to be amused by what Jordan said.

His eyes flick up to mine before dropping again, the smile deepening.

Or maybe he is paying attention to me. He might not have said a word to me this entire day, but that doesn't mean he's completely ignoring my existence.

My stomach tumbles as I look at the crystals. As attractive as Adrian is when he smiles like that—and as comforting and warming as it was to have his arm wrapped around me last night—I can't allow myself to get caught up in it. We're too different. Two house plants requiring completely different conditions to survive. I want meaningful. He wants meaningless. He desires to stay well away from loves steep cliff, I'm still nose-diving over its edge for my ex-boyfriend. If ever there were two people who wouldn't work, it's us.

Except…Last night, as Adrian held me in his arms, I didn't feel a drop of guilt. I was talking about the past, but I felt tethered to the present. To him.

Maybe this is what I need. Maybe now is the time for me to finally move on. Maybe—

No. I derail that train of thought as soon as it finds steam. Even if I did decide to move on, it could never be with Adrian. I will always, always want meaning with the person I'm with, and as far as I'm aware, he never will.

"Are you ever going to buy that?" I hear Evie say.

She's standing by Adrian's side. Both stare into a tall, thin glass cabinet shaped like a grandfather clock, but I can't see what they're looking at because of the stand in front of me.

"I'm not spending forty-pounds on a pen," Adrian

replies.

Evie shakes her head. "You look at that thing every time you come in here. Why don't you just save yourself the misery and buy it?" When Adrian continues to stare at it like he won't budge, she adds, "You'll be devastated when somebody else does. You're lucky it hasn't gone already." She turns, walking away, and I watch for long enough to learn that Adrian walks out without a purchase.

Outside, Christmas stalls line the market square. A crowd of people surround each one, making it the busiest part of town. It seems like everyone has flocked to this spot, but it doesn't surprise me. If Evie hadn't insisted we visit here before leaving, the smell alone would have drawn me in. Apples, cinnamon, mulled cider, roasted hog, something buttery and rich and salty. Roasted nuts, toffee, spiced gingerbread cookies. Hot chocolate and bailies and coffee.

As we pass each stall, I buy enough food to make me feel sick, but it's so good that I keep craving more.

"I'm getting us all a spiced rum," Evie declares after her fourth wine. With a determined look, she grabs Jordan's hand and drags him to a stall that sells booze, leaving me alone with Adrian.

While I've ploughed through all of the delectable food stalls, Adrian has tasted every alcoholic beverage the market has to offer. If it's taught me one thing about him, it's that he must have a high alcohol threshold to still be on his feet. I'd be completely wasted if I were him, probably lying in the grass somewhere slurring words at the sky.

He's standing a little to my side, eyes glazed over, cheeks pink, and there's this smile on his face that makes my heart squeeze.

"What are you smiling about?" I ask.

He turns his smile my way, making the squeeze intensify. "You have crumbs on your coat." He reaches over as if to brush them off, but as I look down, he uses his finger to flick my nose instead, startling me.

The laugh that whispers out of him can only be described as s-e-x-y. I take a few quick breaths before saying, "If you're done being playful." As I swat his hand away, he raises it as if to do the same thing again.

"I like being playful." He taps my nose before adding, "With you."

My pulse jumps.

Okay. I turn my face away. *This is a different side to Adrian.*

Not for the first time today, I see a group of girls trying to make eye contact with him. They stand a little to his side, holding steaming cups of something in their hands, eyeing him like he's something to devour.

When he runs a hand through his hair and peers down at me, I start to think the same thing.

Oh, God. He is *delicious.*

I swallow. "You do realise those girls are staring at you, right?" I have no idea why I'm even bringing them up. "They're dying to get your attention." I nod to his left, but Adrian doesn't budge. His eyes are on me.

"Why would I want their attention when I have yours?"

Stupid. Heart.

It's put on a pair of erratically-beating wings that are setting off into flight.

"I—" I stop whatever it is I'm saying and give myself a moment to clear my head. The thing is, I'm starting to understand why Evie likes to warn her friends away from Adrian. He has…a way about him. A smile that pulls you in while simultaneously cautioning you to stay away. He's a beguiling wolf, ready to disarm you before leaving you in ruin. And I might just be willing to let him. "What about Molly?" I blurt in a moment of swarming panic.

He blinks in genuine confusion. "Molly?"

I don't know why I'm bringing her up. All I know is that if I don't distract him with something, I might fall into his haze, and once I'm there, I'm not sure I'll be able to find my way out again. "Don't you have a thing with her? Evie said you hook up every time you come here. And you stayed at the pub last night to be with her. Before—" Before coming back to the lodge and comforting me with your arms.

His eyes flash, but if he's remembering what I'm remembering, he doesn't say anything about it. "That isn't true. The thing about Molly. We hooked up once, and since then, I've kept it platonic. I stayed with her at the pub last night because I didn't want to —" He cuts off. For one wild moment, I imagine it having something to do with me. "I don't like Molly," he continues, swallowing. "She knows we can't have anything serious."

"Because it can't be anything serious with you?"

I see the moment it happens. The moment my words sober him. I don't even know why I said them. This entire conversation has been something that's gotten away from me—a cart derailing from the road. Adrian stares at me for a long time, and for the life of me, I can't figure out what he's thinking. All I can do is go into defence mode, body tensing as it prepares for a hit.

"Exactly," is all he says.

Just like that, my heart deflates, the wings dropping to ash on either side. The flirty smile is gone from Adrian's face. So, too, are the soft eyes. They've been replaced with straight lines and hard edges.

And I regret it. I *liked* flirty Adrian. Flirty Adrian was fun and non-serious. He made me nervous, sure, but I realise now that it wasn't the bad kind. It was the heart-pinching, breath-holding kind—the excitement before a kiss, the zing from when your crush first touches your hand. But I'm so out of practice with flirting that I let my fear overwhelm me. And now I've chased flirty Adrian away.

Would it be so bad to flirt back? Flirting doesn't need to be serious. It doesn't even need to be meaningful. Seriously, Ophelia, it would have been fun!

Just as I contemplate how to coax flirty Adrian back, Jordan and Evie return with the drinks, and it's like he never existed. A rare version of him that needs to be caught with both hands and held onto.

"For you." Evie holds out a spiced rum with warm apple juice for me to take while Jordan does the same to Adrian.

"I'm good," Adrian says, stepping back with his hands in his pockets.

The regret starts in my chest and lodges in my throat. Not only have I chased Adrian's flirty side away, but I've also made it so that *this* version of him doesn't even want to risk another drink in case it brings him back.

"You're not drinking anymore?" Evie asks. "Why?"

"The alcohol has gotten to my head."

Right. As in: *I flirted with Ophelia. I must be drunk.*

"Then what should I do with this?" Jordan holds up the spare drink. Before I can think about it, I swoop it from his hands, taking a long swig before any of them can react.

The hot liquid crawls down my throat and settles my growing anxiety. I take another long swig. My reasoning for this: maybe if I have a little alcohol buzzing through my system, I'll be able to awaken *my* flirty side, and she'll succeed in bringing back Adrian's.

Only my theory doesn't work in practice. Three drinks later, although I feel pleasantly light and giddy, the alcohol doesn't help with the fact I've forgotten how to flirt. Whenever I come close to feeling brave enough to say something to him, I freeze, and the words stop at my throat. I want to casually nudge his arm and tell him I like to be playful, too. Instead, I give in, and throughout our train journey back to the village, Adrian and I say nothing.

We make it back to the park, navigating the dark with our torches, and I know my chance is gone.

"Let's go for a drink at the bar," Evie says, pulling us all to a stop.

Now deflated, I shake my head. "I'm ready for bed."

"I'll come." It's Adrian who says it. Adrian, who always says no to going to the bar. Adrian, who said no to alcohol earlier on. And Adrian, who, approximately one second before I said no, looked like he wanted to say the word himself.

That thought sobers me completely.

"I guess that means I'll see you all later," I say, knowing that Jordan won't come back without Evie. I start walking, trying to ignore the darkness looming on all sides of me, but Jordan's hand pulls me to a stop.

"We can't let you walk back on your own," he says. "Plus, you're terrified of the dark."

"*Correction*," I wave the torch at him. "I'm scared of complete darkness. This prevents that. And I'll be fine." I hope I sound braver than I feel. In actuality, I wish they'd all walk me back. It's fine here. Here is safe, what with the warm, safe glow from the facilities nearby. But as soon as I look over my shoulder...

A shiver runs through me.

"I'll be fine," I say again. "Nothing to worry about." *So long as a wolf doesn't try to murder me.*

"I'll walk you."

I hear the words, but I have to turn to make sure they came from him.

"You'll walk me?" I repeat, still unconvinced I heard him right.

Adrian looks conflicted like he doesn't really want to walk me back, but he isn't entirely against it, either.

He turns to Evie. "I'll walk Ophelia back to the lodge, and then I'll return for a drink."

"Thank you," she squeals. "Make sure she gets back safely."

A look passes behind his eyes that makes me think if a wolf did cross our paths, he'd throw himself in front of me to keep me from harm.

Unless he's the wolf.

As we walk, our torches barely pierce the space in front of us, so we stay close together, walking slowly thanks to the odd patches of ice.

In the silence, I marvel at how two people can go from baring their souls to each other one day to barely crossing the line of strangers the next. That's what he feels to me now—a stranger. Not a word is exchanged between us. I try to pass it off as us concentrating on the earth beneath our feet, but I can't shake the belief that Adrian is thinking about earlier, and how I'd basically killed the mood. If only I can start something up again—

"Ouch!" My foot slips on some ice I'd been too distracted to notice, and I fall flat on my ass. The landing is painful. And hard. And *cold*.

"Are you alright?" Adrian crouches in front of me, offering me his hands as his torch lands discarded beside him. He sounds concerned, but I can barely make out his face, never mind the expression it's wearing.

"Yup," I grunt as I take his offering. And then I laugh at the admittedly hilarious irony of it all.

"You're laughing?" Now he sounds baffled.

"At my own lack of game, yes."

"Game?" His hands stay holding mine, their grip firm yet gentle.

Now that I see the hilarity of my situation, I don't mind opening up about it. We can share in my foolishness.

"I've been trying to flirt with you," I admit. "But I've forgotten how to flirt. Clearly, I'm much better at falling on my ass and covering myself in twigs."

He's silent for a few moments. Then, "You've been trying to flirt?"

"Yes."

My heart decides that now is the time for it to pound. In the ensuing silence, I wonder if Adrian can hear it. He lowers our hands, thumb brushing over my pulse point in a way that makes my stomach do a loop.

"You're a shit flirter."

Laughter bubbles through me. "I know. That's what I'm saying."

"I didn't even know you were trying to flirt. Are you sure that's what you were doing?"

Taking one hand back, I pinch his arm. "Yes, I'm sure. But, as I've already said, I've forgotten how."

"You haven't *forgotten* how to flirt. Nobody forgets that. You're just nervous."

"Well, we can't all be effortless flirts like you."

"When have you ever seen me flirt, Ophelia?"

Even the way he says my name sounds flirty. "Um, earlier? You were flirting with me at the market?"

He scoffs. "You call *that* flirting? That wasn't flirting. It was merely a tease."

My heart dips at the thought of what his actual flirting must be like if that wasn't it. "Why would I want their attention when I have yours?" I repeat his words back to him. "That was you flirting. Don't deny it."

He picks both of our torches up off the floor, handing mine back to me, and in the new light, I can see the smirk on his lips and catch the glint in his eyes. "Good to know you remember it word for word."

I stare, open-mouthed, as he turns into a walk, but then the fear of Adrian disappearing kicks my feet into motion. "Don't leave me."

He slows his step, aggravatingly confident navigating these dark woods without a guide.

"How are you not afraid?" I ask, nearly stumbling onto my ass again. "Anything could be lurking in these woods."

Adrian aims his torch at the roots in front of me. "I think you're the only thing to fear here."

"That's very funny."

He snorts. "If you think this is scary, you should visit the stargazing site. It's even darker than here."

"That's impossible."

"It's also my favourite place."

I don't miss how he doesn't add a word to the end of that statement. Not, it's my favourite place *here*. But it's his favourite place—as in *ever*.

I'm suddenly reminded of my conversation with Evie when she first gave me a tour of the park. Didn't she say that their mum used to take them to the *Dark Zone* every year, and while Evie didn't enjoy it, Adrian did?

Warmth rushes through me as I realise that not only did Adrian feel comfortable enough bringing it up to me, but he also did so with a smile. "Remind me never to go there alone."

His smile stretches.

After a moment of silence, he says, "Let's say, for argument's sake, that I was flirting with you earlier. How would you flirt back?"

"Huh?"

"Use me as your flirting practice. What would you say?"

"Um…" I try to think of something cute and playful, but in the end, I shake my head. "I can't do this. It's too embarrassing."

"Come on." He nudges my arm. "It's only me. And you've said embarrassing things to me before."

Ignoring the way my stomach swoops at his *it's only me* comment—and how he's right about me saying *plenty* of embarrassing things—I exhale and say, "Alright. How would you start the flirting off?"

He doesn't miss a beat. "Why would I want their attention, Ophelia, when I have yours?"

"So you were flirting earlier?"

"Just go along with it."

I clear my throat. "You want my attention?"

"No." He shakes his head. "You sound like you're doubting yourself. Don't give me a question. Give me a statement."

I try again. "My attention isn't the only thing you have."

"That's good. Now try to sound like you enjoy teasing me."

"I do enjoy teasing you."

"Alright, smart ass. Besides your attention, what else do I have?"

Something about the way he says *smart ass* spurs me on. "Me, if you want it."

"And how can I have you?"

"That depends on how you like it. How do you like it, Adrian?"

When he doesn't respond, I shine the torch on his face, afraid that I've either just a) flirted really badly or b) flirted really, really badly.

But he doesn't look like he wants to laugh at my lame attempts to flirt. He looks...affected.

"Are you flustered?" Surprised, I lean closer, but he turns his face away. "Have I flustered you with my flirting, Adrian?"

"It was hot, alright, Ophelia?" He moves the torch out of his face and adds, "Really fucking hot."

My steps falter. When Adrian looks over and sees that I've stopped, he marches back, holding my shoulders from behind and steering me forward. "What's the matter?" he asks. "Feeling guilty that you caused a man to fluster in the dark?"

Maybe it's the fact he's still admitting to being flustered by me. Maybe it's because the word *hot* still zings through my nerves on a loop. Or maybe it's simply because I'm enjoying myself that I say, "There are other things that can be done in the dark."

He stops steering me. No longer feeling his hands on my shoulders, I turn back, finding that he's the one who's now stopped. There's a look in his eyes that makes something long-dormant roar to life inside me.

"What things can be done in the dark, Ophelia?"

Since when did this become so easy? "No one's around

to see us. Use your imagination."

He takes a step towards me. "Maybe I like the idea of sharing a secret with you."

"You can have me as your secret, Adrian, so long as I don't have to share you."

He takes another step. He's so close now that I have to tilt my head back to look at him. "This is starting to feel dangerous."

I swallow. He's right. This no longer feels like harmless flirting. This feels like the kind that leads somewhere. "Maybe I like danger." My stomach tightens at the thought of him touching me. My skin prickles with the need for it.

Adrian takes another step. I step back. We both keep moving until my back hits the base of a tree, and his body is before me.

If I could breathe, I would. One deep breath will cause my chest to hit his. The thought scares me, but I also want him to be nearer. I want to take one last daring move and pull his body against me so that it's Adrian pinning me here instead of only my will.

"We could do it, you know." His breath whispers across my face, smelling like warm apples and sweet rum. I exhale, but that proves to be a mistake because when my chest hits his, it's nowhere near enough contact, and I'm suddenly afraid of what my hands might do.

"What could we do?" I ask, feeling both fearful and brave enough to enter a battlefield. I look at his lips while my torch hangs discarded by my side. Adrian holds his between us. It shows me the maddening smile that plays on his lips. *So. Damn. Attractive.*

"You say you haven't had sex in almost a year?" His lips tug up as he brings his mouth to my ear. "We could have it right here, right now, against this very tree."

His eyes collide with mine, my skin heating beneath their gaze.

And I want it. My entire body is roaring to life at the thought of having him, all of him, right here, right now. It's as if he's reached inside of me and reignited a fire that's long since been turned to ash. It's a desire that can only be quelled by him—an intensity that almost makes me whimper.

Ten seconds ago, I would have been satisfied with a kiss. Now I know that a kiss won't nearly be enough. The ache I feel needs more. It demands all of him and won't settle for anything less.

How is it that I'm feeling this way?

"Are we still practice flirting?" I whisper, my eyes back on his lips.

"You tell me." He leans closer, lowering his forehead so that it presses against mine.

I swallow. How close do his lips need to be before I break and reach for them? I can feel them tantalising me, their warmth radiating onto my skin.

"How about it, Ophelia?" Adrian doesn't need to speak over a murmur. "Should we do it?"

Shadows cross over his face as he lowers the torch, increasing the feeling of danger. His hand finds mine. Slowly, and with a gentleness that doesn't match the intensity pulsating between us, he raises my hand above my head, entwining our fingers together as he pins them to the tree.

I can feel his pulse against my own, beating just as fast.

"Think about it,"—his nose grazes mine—"you'll be more than satisfied,"—another graze—"the pressure will be gone,"—a third, slower graze—"and nobody needs to know."

I tilt my chin. One more inch and our lips will touch. It's exhilarating. There's a certain pleasure in the torture. Fascination in the tease. Adrian's lips are parted, and it almost feels like a kiss as his breath whispers against my own.

Yet...Something at the back of my brain is begging me to pause. I want to ignore it—want to chastise that part of me for spoiling the fun—but there it goes, waving its red flag in warning.

Adrian doesn't move. I know it's because he's waiting to see if I'll close the distance. He's giving me the final move. A move I almost take. But then I realise what the warning is—it's something he said earlier. *Nobody needs to know.* That's what this will be—sex between two people who will never talk about it again. I might have said earlier that I'll be Adrian's secret, but is that really what I want? No. As fun as this will probably be, I don't want to be vulnerable with someone who might very well forget my existence the next morning.

There's a reason why I haven't listened to the awful advice people give after a break-up. *The best way to get over someone is to get under someone else.* It might work for some people, but I don't think that's the case for me. I think if I got into bed with someone for the sake of it, I'd be gaining short-term satisfaction for long-term regret. Because there's also a reason why I've only ever shared a bed with one person before. That person meant something to me. I loved him, I trusted him, I felt connected to him in a way that went deeper than flesh, and I'm certain that's why I enjoyed it. I'm also certain that I want that again. But I know that if I had sex with Adrian right now, it would mean something to me and absolutely nothing to him.

"Wait." I wish I didn't have to say that word. Adrian's body goes rigid. He stays like that for a moment before leaning back, loosening his grip on my hand as he lowers his. "I—I want meaning." I swallow against the heaviness in my throat. My body doesn't want this. My body wants him. "You said it yourself in the car," I force myself to continue. "I should wait until it means something."

"And it wouldn't mean anything with me," he confirms, but it still stings to hear it. He steps back, taking his warmth with him.

My body screams at me to pull him back, to reignite the fire that he'd started and kiss him until it exhausts me. But—"Because it wouldn't mean anything with you," I confirm. *Because you don't want it to.*

He nods. "Then let's forget this ever happened."

Gingerly, he raises my hand—the one still holding the torch—so that the light is pointing in front of me. It makes my stomach flip, but I tell myself to stop being foolish as he turns and starts walking.

Because if he can so easily forget this happened, it would have meant even less to him than I thought.

CHAPTER NINE

Adrian

Maybe I should get used to not being able to sleep here.

But how can I sleep when I can't stop thinking about the girl in the room next door to me?

I should have known better than to take things as far as I did, but the truth is, I'd been trying to resist Ophelia all day. I'd gotten a little too comfortable when she'd rested her head against my shoulder that night during the movie. I thought that if I ignored her during our trip to town, I'd be able to stop thinking about her.

Turns out, she's impossible to ignore.

And as soon as I had alcohol in my system, she was all I could think about.

Suddenly, all I wanted to do was tease her and watch

her blush. I never imagined she'd want to do those things back.

I was doomed the second she told me she'd been trying to flirt with me.

I was turned on the second she started doing it properly.

I don't know how we went from flirting to me pinning her against a tree so fast. All I know is that I wanted her to the point that it was maddening, and I needed her there, then, no matter the logistics. The unfortunate part is that I thought she wanted me, too.

I want meaning.

How could I forget what she'd told me in the car? The advice I'd given her? She's only ever had sex with one person, and there I was, asking her if she wanted it against a tree.

A fucking. Tree.

No. I'm not surprised she told me to wait. Her first time with someone else—did I really think it would be with me? Did I really think she'd *want* it to be with me?

It wouldn't mean anything with you.

That's a statement I should get used to. But of course it wouldn't have meant anything to her if she had sex with me. Even if, for the first time, it felt like it could have meant something to me.

I hear a door open in the hallway and know, without

a doubt, that it's Ophelia. She's the only one—other than me—who gets up so early. I wonder if she's struggling to sleep, too. More likely, she slept soundly enough that she's managed to get enough hours in and is now wide awake. For a moment, I debate getting up with her to get the awkwardness of last night out of the way, but fuck that.

If I'm going to pretend like last night never happened —which I am—then I need time to help me get over it.

When I finally emerge hours later, it's only after I make certain that Jordan and Evie are up as well. I shower first, towel-drying my hair before making my way into the main living area, where Evie, Jordan, and Ophelia are all sitting by the table.

"You're up late," Evie comments. She drops her spoon, looking suddenly offended. "And, hey! Why didn't you come back to the pub to have a drink with us last night?"

"I felt too tired," I lie, having completely forgotten about it. *And totally head-fucked.* I reach for a bowl, placing it on the counter as I throw a quick glance over at Ophelia.

"Morning," she says, smiling as if nothing noteworthy has passed between us these last twenty-four hours. "Or should I say afternoon?"

My grip slackens on a box of cereal. "Afternoon." Has she actually forgotten about last night, or is she just doing a really good job at pretending?

Alright, I think as I pour myself some cereal. *If she can keep her cool about it, then so can I.*

The chair scrapes as I pull it out from beside her. As I sit, I make a point of looking directly at her, but it turns out to be my downfall because when she meets my gaze, images of last night flood my thoughts, and once they're in, I have no chance of forgetting.

There's her sultry expression. The way her lips had parted as though inviting me in. The heat from her hand as I held it over her head, pinning it to the tree.

I look at the table as my cheeks begin to blaze. It's not that I'm embarrassed, per say. It's more that thinking about last night is making me want her all over again, and if I'm not careful, my thoughts will start moving to other ways I might have her—like against this table.

Fuck, is it hot in here?

"Why are you taking your jumper off?" Evie looks up at me with her mouth ajar. "We've only just switched the heating on."

Considering she's dressed in her fluffy onesie, Jordan in his grandad jumper, and Ophelia basically in her coat, I can appreciate why she's surprised.

"Yeah. I—er—run hot." I catch Ophelia's eyes. There's a flush on her face that makes me wonder if she's thinking about the same things as me. If she's turned on by the thought of last night.

Of course she isn't, you asshole.

She wants sex that's meaningful to her. As she pointed out, that isn't with you.

My appetite slowly recedes as disappointment sits in my stomach. I realise that I *want* her to want it with me. I want to be the one who helps her move on. Even more surprising, I want to experience meaningful sex—whatever that is—with her and her alone. I might never have had it before, but I have a feeling that it'd be pretty fucking phenomenal.

Or maybe that isn't what I want. Maybe I'm out of my damn mind. There's a very real possibility that I'm just feeling these things because she's someone I can't have. After all, I haven't known her for long. How could she possibly mean anything to me?

And do I really want the sex to mean anything? I've never wanted that before. I don't even want it now. No. I just want sex. I've tricked myself into thinking otherwise because I know that's what she wants, and I want her. But with meaning comes the burden of caring. I do not want to care about this girl. I certainly don't want the responsibility for her feelings when she's already been hurt.

"You haven't even noticed the presents," Evie complains.

"What presents?" I look around the room, spotting a small pile of gifts in the corner by the TV. I know immediately which ones are Evie's—she always wraps them impeccably, topped with a pretty, frivolous bow that goes straight in the trash. The badly wrapped ones must be Jordan's, which means...

I look at Ophelia, catching her guilty expression. "I haven't put anything there."

"Makes me feel a lot better about not getting any, either." I swivel back to the table as Evie's lips jut into a pout.

"You haven't got me a present?"

"You know I don't do Christmas shopping." I can't think of anything more depressing than joining the chaos outdoors as people rush to buy something they don't even know the other person will like. Visiting town yesterday was bad enough, but I did that with the mindset that it wasn't Christmas shopping, and even then, I had to fight the urge to slip away.

"But I thought we were celebrating Christmas this year?" she continues to sulk.

"I've only just decided that, Evie." My sister is many good things, but her high expectations are a personality fault. Just because I'm open to celebrating Christmas doesn't mean I'll be donning a jumper with Santa's face on it. Evie will think that I will. Never mind the fact that my heart still clenches whenever I walk into the lodge and see the decorations for the first time. Or that the hands on the clock are fast approaching tomorrow.

I shove the thought of tomorrow firmly aside. If I allow it in, I'll drown faster than a hole shovelled in the sand.

"I suppose you do spoil me on my birthdays," Evie allows.

"See? And I'm not the only one who hasn't brought presents." A nod at Ophelia. "There's another persecutor at this table."

"Hey." Ophelia holds her hands up in defence. "That's only because my gift is too obvious. I'll give Jordan and Evie theirs on the day."

"Traitor," I mutter, making her laugh. I don't like what the sound does to me. It zings through my system, giving me the absurd thought that I'd like to hear it again. Not just hear it—but be the cause of it.

"Do you remember how Mum used to hide our presents around the lodge for us to find?" Evie reminisces. "And how we'd make it into a scavenger hunt as we searched for them?"

I smile even as my chest aches. "Yeah." The memory is bittersweet—as it always is when I think about Mum. I loved that woman. I miss her as much today as I did the day we lost her.

But the ache in my chest doesn't feel as sharp as usual. I test its edges, finding it painful but bearable, which is never the case at this time of the year.

It feels completely foreign to me that I'm able to breathe, smile, and say, "And she used to make that God-awful wild-berry pie for breakfast every Christmas morning."

"She did!" Evie tips her head back and laughs. "She was great at baking everything else. Why did she always fail with the pie?"

"Wild-berry pie?" Ophelia questions, eyes flicking between us.

"She used to pick berries on her walk back from the beach and bake them into a pie," Evie answers. "It was *awful*."

"But it marked the start of Christmas day," I add with a small smile. "Shit pie."

"Shit pie." Evie sighs, her eyes drifting off to something I can't see, a memory that belongs only to her.

"She sounds like a phenomenal woman."

My eyes flick over to Ophelia's. Her smile is encouraging, and it makes my heart swell to my throat.

It also makes me wonder about the last time Evie and I smiled within these walls. How long ago it was. It can't have been when Mum was still here, can it? But when I think back, I can't recall a single moment when I've been happy here without her.

And now, here we are, laughing in her memory.

"Excuse me for a second." Pushing out my chair, I go to the bathroom, clutching the sink as I look in the mirror. I got my blue eyes from my mum. They're my favourite thing about myself, even if I do have a stray tear falling from one of them now.

I wipe it aside, thinking about Ophelia and how she wants to love again even though it has, and can still, hurt her.

I wonder if I should be the same.

But even if I wanted to be like her, I still don't know how she does it. For so long, remembering my mum has been akin to opening a door for anxiety and grief to come inside. I don't want more of that. I don't want to fall in love with someone just for them to leave me.

"Are you okay?"

I swivel, finding Ophelia at the door that I left ajar. "I'm fine," I lie.

Her eyes scan my face. "Evie's about to set out the plan for today."

"Oh yeah? What do you think she'll have us do? Hunt down reindeer for dinner?"

Her laugh is the exact sound I wanted to hear again earlier. "More like nurse injured reindeer back to health."

When she meets my eyes with a grin, it happens again. Images of last night barrel into me. But it isn't the same as earlier. This time, I *am* embarrassed. Embarrassed that I thought, for a single second, that Ophelia would want to have sex with me.

Because even if—and it's a very big if—I ever did decide to fall in love, a girl like her could never love me back.

Ophelia's smile falters. I open my mouth to bring up last night, to apologise for my part in it, but I'm interrupted.

"You guys!" Evie calls. "Come on! The clock is ticking!"

Looking like she wants to say something to me, too, Ophelia quickly turns, leaving before I have the chance to ask for a word later.

"Okay." To the middle of the table, Evie pushes a piece of paper that's been scrawled on in her handwriting. "Here's the plan." She ticks the list off on her fingers. I stop listening, thinking instead about how I might start off my apology to Ophelia. I know I told her to forget about last night, but there's no way I can stop that memory from resurfacing. As it stands, I know I was wrong. I pushed it too far. Disregarded all that she'd told me in the car. For that, I *need* to let her know I'm sorry. I need her to know that I'm not a complete asshole. I fight the urge to look over at her as Evie continues, but

I can see her nodding her head to everything my sister is saying. One glance, and I'm afraid I won't be able to look away again. "And then we'll end the night at the Christmas Eve Eve party," Evie finishes.

I flinch. It's involuntary. But hearing the words *Christmas* and *Eve* together will always strip away my self-control.

"Right then." Evie pulls the paper towards her and neatly folds it. "Let's go."

"Where are we going?" I ask.

She throws me a look. "Were you not listening to a word I just said? We're taking one of the trails to the beach, and then we're visiting the lighthouse."

"Oh." I nod like I was listening after all. "Alright."

As I walk over to the coat stand, I try to brush the thought of tomorrow away from my mind. I'm not ready to think about it. Not yet.

Right now, I have another worry on my mind.

CHAPTER TEN

I've spent the entire morning trying to pretend like last night never happened, just like Adrian wanted.

I did a pretty good job to begin with, but that was before he decided to finally stroll out of bed. When he ambled into the kitchen with his shaggy hair wet from the shower, that's when I knew I was hopeless. Because it's one thing controlling my mind. It's another controlling a body that has its own agenda.

When I first laid eyes upon him, my body reacted. It *wanted* Adrian last night. More so than it's wanted any one person for a long time. It wanted him so much that it would have taken him against a *tree*, for crying out loud. The crazy part is that I think my mind started wanting him, too.

I pull on my trainers and try to remember to forget

last night ever happened.

It. Did. Not. Happen.

"Are you trying to ruin your only pair of shoes?"

Stumbling, I look up to find Adrian beside me. Yes, I'm pulling on my shoes with a little more force than necessary, but I didn't think anyone was watching.

"These trainers have been through more ordeal than this. Besides," I turn my back to him. "I'm tired."

It frustrates me that Adrian was able to sleep in past noon. After we returned to the lodge last night, he went straight to his room, as did I. Only I didn't sleep. I spent most of the night trying to forget our almost-kiss, which, of course, can be added to my list of failures.

I use the wall to hold my balance, struggling as the back of my trainer refuses to cooperate. Adrian reaches for my elbow, steadying me himself. "Thank you," I say, hating the way my body reacts to something so simple as his touch.

As I stand, my eyes collide with the gleaming blue of his, and just like earlier, my thoughts begin to race, powering through every image I've tried to erase.

His hands, pinning me to a tree. The feel of rough bark against my knuckles and smooth skin against my palms. The quick *thrum-thrum* of two racing hearts. The heat from his body as my own temperature rises, wanting him, *needing* him, ready to welcome him. The lips that were waiting for me to touch them.

"Can I talk to you for a second?" he murmurs.

The all-too-familiar butterflies swarm in my stomach. "What about?"

He looks over my shoulder, probably to make sure Jordan and Evie have left the lodge, before leaning closer. "I'm sorry about last night."

I might register the meaning behind his words if it weren't for my body reacting again. My heart is pounding. His nearness is giving me warmth against the cold, and it's all too easy to lean a little closer...

"Ophelia?"

"Hmm?"

"I said I'm sorry. About last night."

"Oh." I blink as if breaking from a trance. Adrian leans back, his brows creasing in concern. That's when I realise the magnitude of his words—that he's acknowledging last night happened, and he hasn't forgotten at all. "I thought you wanted to forget about it?"

"Had *you* forgotten about it?"

The intensity in his eyes surprises me. It's almost as if...but no. He *wanted* me to forget.

"I hadn't forgotten," I admit.

Again, his eyes betray another emotion. Or am I imagining the triumph there?

"I hadn't forgotten, either," he says. "And I was wrong to take it so far. I'm sorry about that."

He's *apologising* for it? "I let it go that far, too. You don't need to be sorry."

He shakes his head. "No. I'm the one who—" He looks over my shoulder again before leaning closer. "The one who suggested we have sex against a tree." He says the words so quietly, I swear the other two wouldn't hear even if they were right behind me. "If I'd been using my brain, I never would have done that."

I flinch. In other words, it wasn't his brain that wanted to have sex with me. "It's fine. It wouldn't have meant anything to you. We stopped it when we should."

He gives me a strange look. "To me? Are you saying that it would—"

"Are you two coming or not?" Jordan interrupts.

"We should go." I look at Adrian and away again. "Apology accepted."

The afternoons are getting colder. I can feel the frost in the air, biting my nose and nipping at my cheeks. I watch Jordan and Evie ahead of me, huddling together to keep each other warm. It reminds me of the warmth I felt from Adrian, and for a second, I imagine having his arms wrapped around me, heating me like a furnace, but I quickly shove that thought into oblivion.

I'm not ready for it yet, anyway. No way. My body

might have roared to life beneath his touch yesterday, but I can't let it confuse me. It's like Adrian said—it's his body that wants me. Not his brain. And I'm not ready to move on.

Am I?

I know that I've not been ready to move on before now, but the thing is, I think I'm starting to *want* to move on, even if the thought of doing so still brings panic to my chest.

I want to feel the weight of a hand holding mine. I want to feel the gentle touch of fingers against my skin. I want the steady assurance that comes from when you know someone as well as yourself and the safety you feel when your eyes meet theirs from across a crowded room.

I want the excitement you feel when you hear their car pull up on the driveway and the complete ease from when you awake to their body next to yours. I want the anxiety of checking for a pulse when they're sleeping and the gratitude from when you feel it, that precious thing, the most beautiful beat in the world.

I want to love someone again and give them my endless support and encouragement. My friendship. I want to love someone so much that I'll fight in their corner no matter what weapon is used on the other side.

But...how do I go from loving someone as much as

I did to giving that love to somebody else? Is it even possible?

When the others stop walking, I stop, too, but I've been so caught up in the labyrinth of my own mind that I have no idea where we are or why we've stopped.

"The view's beautiful here, isn't it?"

Looking to my right, I find Adrian beside me, staring off at something ahead.

"Beautiful," I agree before I even know what I'm saying it about.

He catches me staring at him, so I quickly look away, seeing for the first time why we've stopped. Ahead of us, farmland spreads far and wide, and beyond that, the sprawling grey of the sea.

"Beautiful," I say again with meaning.

"The train is coming!" Evie claps her hands together as she leans forward, peering down what I realise is a train track. I hear it then. The *chug chug* of an approaching train. The steam can be seen in the distance, but it doesn't explain why it has Evie so excited. "Just wait until you see this," she says, looking over her shoulder at us. "It's what we'll be going on later."

As the train makes its slow journey past us, I realise why Evie clapped in excitement. The entire train has been decorated with Christmas lights, illuminating each carriage so they shine as bright as a shop window. I marvel for a single moment before I look over my shoulder at Adrian. I'm not surprised to find that he isn't watching the train. Instead, he's standing away from us, eyes pressed against a pay-to-view telescope aimed at the water.

I walk towards him, hands burrowed deep into my pockets. "Searching for drowning reindeer?"

His lips twitch. "What else?" Moving his eyes from the glass, he looks over at me. "Want to take a look?"

He steps aside, letting me take his place, but when I crouch down to press my eyes to the glass, all I see is a black screen like something is covering it. I give Adrian a questioning look, half-convinced he's covering it with his hand, but he holds a pound coin out for me to see. Slotting it into the machine with a smirk, he indicates for me to try again.

"Thank you." This time, when I press my eyes to the glass, I find the sea before me, sprawling water bobbing in differing shades of grey. It looks as if it's right before me, like if I reached out my hand, I'd feel the cold water against my fingers—

"You know you can't actually touch it, right?" he asks.

I pull my hand back. "I had to try."

Something touches the small of my back. Adrian's hand. He uses his other one to gently guide the telescope to the right. "Look over here." He stops when it's no longer the water I'm looking at but a solitary lighthouse sitting on jutting rocks. "Do you see it?" he whispers.

Goosebumps rise where his breath touches my neck. "I see it," I whisper back.

His fingers move, applying gentle pressure. "Every year," he murmurs, "I come to this spot just to see it. And every year, it takes my breath away."

I turn to face him, regretting it when his hand falls. "You like lighthouses?"

"I do. There's something..." His lips pucker. "*Solitary* about them that I admire."

"I like them, too, pretty much for the same reason." My eyes move towards it. Without the telescope, it's just a sharp spike in the sky. Mysterious and spectacular and entirely alone. "Sometimes, I find myself daydreaming about escaping to one. You know, living there. Just me and the lighthouse and no one around."

When I turn to Adrian, I find him watching me with a peculiar look in his eyes. "I dream about the same thing."

"What are you two talking about?"

I startle when I realise Jordan has joined us. He has his hands in his pockets, eyes flicking between us.

"Just a mutual love for lighthouses," Adrian says, giving me a secret smile.

The afternoon isn't nearly as enjoyable as I'm sure

Evie wants it to be. It is far too cold to be walking along the beach, and as soon as we admit this to ourselves, we make an early escape, buying four steaming cups of coffee at the village café. The ride on the Christmas train is a highlight, so I'll give Evie that—a woman pushing a trolley brings round mince pies and hot chocolate with marshmallows on top—but since we can't see the decorations on the inside, it's just like any ordinary train.

When we arrive back at the lodge, Jordan cracks open a beer. Evie follows him by pouring herself a gin, and even Adrian makes himself a whisky on the rocks.

I look at each of them before shrugging my shoulders. "Since it seems to be the thing around here." Opening a bottle of Sauvignon, I pour myself a glass, bringing it to my lips as I catch Adrian's eyes.

"Giving in to peer pressure?" he teases.

I lower the glass. "It's either that or face the wrath of Evie for not joining in."

He nods in sudden seriousness. "You're right. My sister is terrifying when she's angry."

"Hey!" Evie looks at us both in affront. "I'm only a little bit scary."

"If you think Evie's scary," Jordan says with a pointed look at me, "you should see Ophelia when she's in one of her moods. Now *that's* terrifying."

"I can't imagine you in a mood." Adrian tilts his head as he examines me. "How moody do you get?"

Jordan is the one who answers. "Imagine daggers for eyes and a chill whenever she looks at you. I once made her so mad that she literally shook. I thought there was an earthquake."

"I'm not that bad," I say, but there's enough bite in my words for my brother that Adrian raises a brow. "I'm not," I add, desperate now. "Really."

"Whatever you say, Ophelia." Adrian downs his whisky before walking to my side and pouring himself another. He's wearing that infuriating smile—the one that makes me want to put an elbow to his ribs.

Choosing sweetness over violence, I smile and say, "Don't make my temper flare, Adrian. You'll regret it."

His smile widens. "Maybe that's what I want."

I take a sip of my wine, feeling a fuzziness that I know I can't yet blame on the alcohol. Taking my glass over to the sofa, I feel a buzz when Adrian follows.

He sits closer to me than he usually would with Jordan and Evie in the room, but it's still far away enough that no part of us touches. Still, it feels like he's seconds away from leaning in. Or seconds away from pinning my hands to a tree.

I'm doing a terrible job at forgetting last night happened.

"I should probably start getting ready." Needing escape, I dart to my feet, grabbing the bottle of white and taking it with me to my room. My heart thrashes when I hear footsteps behind me.

"I'm coming with you."

I breathe when I realise it's Evie.

"Figured I should do my make-up before I'm too drunk to care," I tell her.

She laughs. "I once went out with one eyebrow unfinished because the alcohol hit me too fast. All I wanted to do was go out and dance."

I look at the bottle in my hand. "Maybe I should save this for later? I'm not sure I can pull the one-eyebrow look off."

"We're all getting drunk tonight, anyway. It's been decided." Looping her arm through mine, she walks with me into my room. "What are you wearing?"

"The only dress I brought." As she plops onto my bed, I pull the dress from my suitcase and hold it up for her to see. "It'll be okay, won't it?"

"*Y-e-s.*" She runs her hand down the maroon chiffon material. "You're going to look so pretty in this."

After bringing her make-up into my room, we sit cross-legged on the floor, music playing softly in the background as our glasses quickly empty.

"I'm tipsy," I admit as I wriggle into my dress. "Does

this look okay?"

Evie turns, her mouth dropping open as she looks me up and down. "Wow, Ophelia. I didn't think it would look this sexy."

"You're making me blush," I laugh.

She hops to her feet, steering me towards the mirror. "Just *look* at yourself in this. You look amazing!"

I tilt my head, examining my reflection. The dress *is* pretty—light and airy, flowing down to my calves with a sweetheart neckline that makes my breasts look bigger than they are. "Not bad," I nod.

"Not bad?" Evie gapes. "Why have you never worn this before?"

I take a deep breath, holding it in before I let it out again. The truth is, I bought this dress a while ago, back when I thought I had a reason to celebrate. But then the break-up happened, and I haven't felt the urge to wear it since. Even now, I'm half-torn between yanking it off and throwing it in the fire. But…I want to look nice tonight.

Adrian and Jordan are sitting near each other when we head back, heads bent over one of their phones. They laugh simultaneously, and I pause, unused to seeing Adrian with such mirth on his face. Leaning against the doorway, I watch as the laughter continues, a smile curling up my lips.

"What are you two laughing at?" Evie asks, interrupting their moment as she strolls to their side.

I stand upright as Adrian's eyes drift right past her, landing on me. I might be embarrassed at getting caught staring if it weren't for the way his eyes move downward—slowly—taking in my dress and its sweetheart neckline. They flick up again, meeting my eyes and holding them.

My entire body prickles as though seared by his gaze.

"You look nice." The words come from Jordan. Thankfully, he's too busy gawking at Evie to notice how I've been staring at her brother and how he's been staring at me.

"Thank you," Evie says, cheeks flushing pink. She's wearing a short black skirt with sheer tights, a black baby-dol top, and a denim jacket to give the look more of an edge. "You look nice, too."

Jordan stands, walking over and pecking her cheek with a kiss.

It's such a sweet act that I feel a pang in my chest that's both painful and wonderful. The pain is because I remember a time when I used to get kissed like that, but it's wonderful because Jordan has finally found someone who makes him happy, and for that, I can only be grateful.

Adrian clears his throat. "We should get going." As

he stands, my eyes absorb what he's wearing, from the white cotton shirt tucked into grey checkered trousers to the brown leather belt buckled at his waist.

Ho-ly mother of sex appeal.

I'm well aware that I'm staring at him again, but it takes a colossal amount of effort to tear my eyes away. Even when I'm safely staring at a wall instead of him, I have to fight the urge to look back. Because Adrian in a hoodie and jeans is one thing. Adrian in trousers and a shirt...

I scurry over to the coat stand.

"You look nice, too." The words barely carry over a whisper, but I still jump out of my skin as Adrian steps beside me. He smirks as if he knows the effect he's having on me, reaching around me to grab his jacket in a way that brings him just about close enough to brush my arm.

I might move out of his way if I weren't still startled by his words. I might say the same thing back if it weren't for *nice* not even scratching the surface of how Adrian looks tonight. And why does he have to smell so good? Like saffron and apples and something distinctly woodsy.

Resisting the urge to gawk at him some more, I circle around him and pull on my coat. My excitement for the night is steadily building, and I want to hold on to this feeling. I want to cherish it and encourage it and keep the momentum moving.

More than anything, I want to find Adrian alone and learn all the ways to make his heart race as fast as mine.

CHAPTER ELEVEN

The party is in full swing by the time we arrive.

Evie tells me the locals wait all year for this party, which is why they go all out with the decorations, music, and food. Nearly everyone in here is donning a Santa hat, including the DJ. At the main bar, there's already a huge queue. There are also other makeshift bars propped up like a movie set dotted around —one for champagne, one for hot drinks, even one for craft beer.

A man dressed in a full Santa costume walks past us, frothing pint glass held high, followed closely by a man dressed as a reindeer.

"Well, if this doesn't make you want to puke," Adrian says.

Thinking this is probably close to punishment for him, I eye him sideways, but the small smile he gives me tells me he's handling it well.

"I've internally puked twice already," I tell him, making his smile widen.

Deciding that we want to go fancy this evening, Evie and I leave the two boys for the champagne bar, diving head-first into the crowd. When we finally get to the point of being served, we order two glasses each, saving the need to queue up again so soon.

They aren't there when we return to the spot we left them.

"Where do you think they've gone?" I ask, incapable of searching over the tops of people's heads, even on my tiptoes.

"Not a clue." Evie looks unconcerned as she sips her champagne. "Let's just find a seat and hope they make their way over to us." With skill, she manages to navigate us to a free bench by the wall, our champagne glasses *dinging* on the table in front of us. "Cheers," she says, holding a glass out to me.

"Cheers." We clink glasses before taking one sip, and then another, and then another. When my first glass is empty, I turn to Evie with a fuzzy smile and say, "I forgot how quickly champagne gets to my head."

"Me too," she giggles. "And let's not forget that bottle of wine."

It's probably nowhere near as funny as we're making

it out to be, but soon, we're both laughing into each other's laps.

"I'm so glad you invited me here," I say, feeling the energy from the room buzzing through my veins. "I wasn't sure about it at first, but it's the best decision I've made this year."

"I'm happy you came here, too." Evie wraps her arms around me, suddenly emotional. "You're like family to me, Ophelia."

"We *are* family." I give her a squeeze. "I've never seen Jordan as happy as he is with you. I consider you a sister."

"*Aw*. And I've never been as happy as I am with Jordan." She leans back with a sniff, wiping a tear from her eye before looking at me. Something shifts in her expression. It's like she wants to say something to me but isn't sure if she can. "Speaking of happy," she starts, "I've never seen Adrian smile so much, either. As his sister, I'm pretty sure it's because of you."

My heart does a quick rise before falling into a sharp drop. What she's saying is a nice sentiment, so why doesn't it match the look she's giving me?

"Is that a bad thing?" I ask.

"No." She shakes her head. "But I do need to warn you about something." Again, she pauses, scanning my face like she's torn between saying whatever it is she wants to say or leaving it to the will of fate. "Adrian is a really bad person to fall for," she decides to tell me.

I open my mouth and close it. Really, I have no words for that.

"Don't get me wrong," she quickly continues. "He's a really great brother and all. I just wouldn't recommend him in the romance department."

Oh no.

Oh no, no, no.

I know what she's doing. She's giving me *The Speech* —the one Adrian warned me about. Which means she thinks I'm in danger of falling for him.

"I'm not falling for Adrian," I say, wanting—*needing*— her to believe it. "Seriously. I'm the last person you need to be giving this advice to."

"I thought that." Her eyes have taken on a different expression. Concern mixed with regret. "Believe me, I never thought I'd need to say this to you. But then I sometimes catch the way you look at him, and the way he looks at you. But my brother, he—" She cuts herself off before starting again. "He's never had a girlfriend before, and I don't think he ever will." Her voice softens as her words stick to the air between us, making it thick and uncomfortable. "I just don't want to see you hurt again, Phi."

I flinch. It's the way she says my name. It's not only a

reminder of all the hurt I've felt this year—a hurt I'm not sure I've yet healed from—but also a reminder that I can be hurt like that again.

"I'm not falling for Adrian," I repeat. My stomach is no longer a home for giddy butterflies but a bed for twisted thorns. "I'm still not ready to move on." The thorns sharpen as I repeat the phrase I've been saying to myself over and over for almost a year. *I'm not ready. I'm not ready. I'm not ready.* Is it the type of thing that if I say it enough, I'll stop knowing if I *am* ready?

I think about Adrian, *really* think about him, and start to wonder if moving on is possible.

He's never had a girlfriend before.

Wouldn't it just be tragic if the first person I've managed to feel something for is someone who isn't available?

It would be nice to think that knowing about Adrian's history is enough to keep my feelings at bay. But I know all about the chaotic nature of falling for someone. It happens despite warnings, boarded-up windows, and locked-away hearts.

"Enough boy talk." Evie taps a finger against one of her empty glasses. "Let's get two more of these."

It's during our fourth champagne when we finally find Jordan, who tells us he's had two shots and two glasses of whisky.

"You weren't kidding when you said you're getting drunk tonight, huh?" I eye my brother up and down, noticing the docile smile on his face that marks the beginnings of him being drunk.

"Is my brother as drunk as you?" Evie asks.

Jordan grins. "No idea. The last time I saw him was when he left me to talk to Molly."

Again, my heart does a sharp nosedive into my stomach, but I ignore it.

"Who's coming to the dancefloor with me?" I ask, deciding that I'm just about drunk enough to make a fool out of myself by dancing. Thankfully, so are Jordan and Evie, but dancing with them basically means I'm dancing alone. I'm not drunk enough for *that* not to be awkward—third-wheeling has never been a comfort of mine—so I start shimmying my way off the floor, where I'm intercepted by a tall frame.

For a second, my heart stops, imagining Adrian in front of me, but when I look up, it isn't him. It takes me a moment to place who it is, but I recognise him from the pub we went to after we arrived—Molly's cousin.

"Having a good night?" Molly's cousin calls over the music.

"Yeah," I call back. "Thanks." Not wanting to refer to him as Molly's cousin, I add, "Sorry. What was your name again?"

"Oh, so you remember my face?" He grins. "The name's Eric."

"Mine's Ophelia."

"I remember." The smile he's giving me should probably make me feel something, but there's nothing there. Just a wide expanse of no-feeling. "Do you want to sit down?" he asks. "Or do you want to keep dancing?"

"Sit, for sure." Third-wheeling is one thing. Dancing as a couple might just be worse.

We find a table on the edge of the dancefloor, our chairs pushed close together thanks to the venue cramming as many tables in as possible. "Are *you* having a good night?" I ask, realising that I didn't ask that earlier.

"I am now." Eric grins again. My brain registers that he's being flirtatious, but no part of me can muster up the fluttering sensation I'd felt when Adrian did it.

Adrian, who I haven't seen since arriving.

I search the floor for him, sweeping swiftly past it when I realise dancing is the last thing Adrian will be doing, scanning the tables instead. My heart stops when I find him on a table across from ours.

He looks just as damn sexy as he did back at the lodge, except now his hair is more ruffled, which only adds to his appeal.

The fluttering comes in full force when his eyes lift,

colliding with mine. He's not even shameful about it, whereas I'm suddenly struggling to breathe.

My eyes dart to the table, and when I peek back up, he's still looking at me. I notice Molly in the seat beside him, tugging his arm as she tries to grab his attention, but his eyes don't move.

"So are you here for the New Year?" Eric asks, successfully making me jolt as I remember his existence. "Sorry," he laughs. "I didn't mean to scare you."

"No. It's okay. I scare easily," I lie. Feeling foolish, I turn my back on Adrian and give Eric my full attention. "No to the New Year. We leave the day after Boxing Day."

"Oh." His brows draw together. "That's a shame." After a moment, he adds, "You're here with Adrian, aren't you?" Before I can answer that question, he throws another one at me. "Is he your boyfriend?"

"No." The word shoots out faster than I would have liked. "I mean, I've only just met him."

Relief lifts his brows. "Oh. That's cool." I'm not sure what's *cool* about it, but if he wants to describe it as that. "I thought you might have been an item after seeing how you were the other day."

"How we were?"

"You know. You looked kinda close."

You should look at the table across the floor. I'm no

160

different from your cousin.

"Anyway," he laughs a little awkwardly as he shuffles closer. "Have you enjoyed your time here? I haven't scared you away, have I?" He adds this with a teasing smile, but again—no flutters.

What is wrong with me? He's an attractive man. He's nice. He's interested. Why can't I feel at least something?

"I've enjoyed myself." My mind travels to Adrian again. Which, I tell myself, makes complete sense since I have spoken to him the most, and he has been a highlight. That doesn't mean I'm in any danger of falling for him.

It gets harder to convince myself I feel nothing for Adrian as Eric continues asking me questions. Despite my conscious effort not to look, my eyes drift over my shoulder, and every time I look at him, Adrian looks back, shooting a thrill through my veins. I take another sip of my drink, trying to clear my thoughts, but the alcohol does nothing to assist with that. A giddiness sizzles beneath my skin like it's waiting to burst.

"Ophelia?"

"Sorry?" I force myself to refocus on Eric, finding him watching me like he's waiting for an answer.

"Do you want a drink?"

"Oh." Realising how drunk I now feel, I say, "Would you mind getting me a water?"

"Not at all." As he heads to the bar, I feel a sudden exposure. It's like having Eric with me offered a safety cushion between Adrian and me, and with him gone, I'm afraid to look over my shoulder.

Even with the fear, my eyes have a will of their own, lifting against my control as if drawn by a force that can't be fought. When they find Adrian this time, a hammer hits my chest, stopping the mechanics of my heart. Instead of looking back at me, he has his neck bent towards Molly's, their lips locked together.

I'm frozen. I watch in that way when you don't want something to be real, so you keep watching in the hopes that it'll somehow change what you're seeing. But this is real. It is happening. Adrian is making out with Molly, and I'm sitting like a fool caught in a net, wanting to escape but flailing helplessly as I watch instead.

Adrian's eyes open, shooting straight to me and widening a fraction. I pierce the table with my stare, trying to keep my cheeks from blazing at being caught watching, but it's hot, hot, hot in here. When did it get so hot? And where is Eric with the water? I need to cool down before I begin sweating from every pore. I need my heart to stop racing. I need to burn the image of Adrian kissing Molly from my memory before I start admitting it bothers me.

Picking up the nearest beermat, I fan my face. I'm still

in the process of doing this when Eric finally returns, his frame casting a shadow over the table.

"Getting a little hot, are we?"

The beermat drops. My eyes shoot to Adrian, finding him leaning against the chair instead of Eric.

"What are you doing here?" My eyes dart to his now vacant table and back again. "You were over there."

"I came to give you company." He turns the chair, sitting so that his body faces mine. "You don't mind, do you?"

"Eric is sitting there."

"I'm sure he won't have a problem with me keeping his seat warm for him." He plays with the rim of my champagne flute, watching me like he's waiting for me to make the next move.

"Shouldn't you be with Molly?" I bristle, pulling the glass away from him. The question is immature, I know, but it annoys me how he's sitting here like he wasn't making out with her mere moments ago. "You seemed to be getting along fine with her."

"Talking to her helped me..." He tilts his head. "Stay away from someone else."

My heart thuds, thuds, thuds. "Who were you trying to stay away from?"

His smile says he has a secret he might be willing to share. "You already know who. She's the girl I wanted to kiss last night." *Thump thump. Thump thump. Thump thump.* Can he hear the effect he's having on me? His smile deepens like he can. "Were you jealous when you saw me kissing her?" he asks, and I can see the genuine curiosity on his face.

"No."

My lie must be obvious because something like triumph flashes behind his eyes. "I wanted it to be with you."

"You—what?"

"I wanted the kiss to be with you." He leans back, and one by one, the butterflies that deserted earlier make a spectacular return, swarming in my stomach like they've brought their friends to the party.

"Then you should never have kissed Molly." I want my disapproval to be heard, but all I sound is breathless.

Adrian surprises me with a frown. "I know. I've been talking to her tonight because I've needed a distraction from you, but I never meant for it to go that far. She leaned in to kiss me, and I thought it would be a good moment to test something."

"Test something?"

The way he looks at me makes my heart work harder. "Whether I could enjoy it."

Thump thump. Thump thump. Thump thump.

"And did you? Enjoy it?"

His smile is so small it almost isn't there. "Like I said. I wanted it to be with you."

What is happening? Is the alcohol getting to my head? Because despite what I told Evie earlier about not falling for her brother, all I want is for Adrian to move closer. To touch me. It doesn't even need to be a kiss. Just a brush of the hand will be enough to ease this craving.

He looks at me like he did last night. Like he's waiting for me to make a move.

"We can't." My words come out in a whisper because, really, I don't want to be saying them. Just like I didn't last night when he had me pinned against the tree. Not kissing him right now goes against everything I'm feeling, but in the back of my brain, I know it's the right choice. Because Adrian's views towards love haven't changed. Neither have mine.

Leaning back, Adrian levels a look at me. "But what if we could? What if it meant something to both of us? What would happen then?"

I know what he's doing. He's asking me to imagine a version of us that isn't real. One where this can lead somewhere.

And I want it enough that I'm willing to go down that path with him.

"Then we would be kissing already."

His eyes glint. "I'd run my free hand through your

hair. The other would be pinning you to that wall over there."

My stomach turns to liquid. "I'd press my body against yours. Invite you to feel me."

"I'd forget the existence of everyone else in here as I rip your clothes off."

"I'd do the same to you."

He leans closer. "I'd taste you first. Make you moan my name before I give you release."

My loins turn to flames. It makes it difficult to remember why I'm not just doing it. Why I'm not closing the distance between us instead of widening it. "I'd bring you back to this chair," I say. "Lower myself slowly over you until it drives you so mad, you slam my hips down and scream out *my* name."

His eyes flare. I can tell he didn't expect me to say it, and I wonder briefly why I'm not embarrassed. But this is Adrian—a guy I've confessed enough things to this week to know that I could probably tell him anything.

I lean forward, blood rushing as he does the same. "What a shame it is that it can only be in our imagination."

His breathing gets heavier. My heart pounds. He opens his mouth, but before he can get past the four syllables of my name, a shadow passes over us. I think I might stay staring at Adrian for longer if it weren't for the sound of a throat clearing.

I bolt upright. Before us, Eric stands with the glass of water.

"The queue was long," he says, eyes darting between Adrian and me with his mouth agape. It's the look that does it for me. Finally embarrassed, I try to act like he hasn't just intruded on me dirty-talking with Adrian.

"Thank you," I say, but Eric isn't looking at me. He's staring at Adrian like he either wants to punch him or make him disappear.

"You're in my seat," is all he says.

Adrian stands. That he does so without confrontation might surprise me if it weren't for the way his blue eyes have stayed locked on mine this entire time.

"For the record," he says like we're the only two here, "the kiss would have meant something to me." He looks at Eric and back again. "And I was jealous, too." With that comment, he turns and walks away, disappearing around the bar.

I stare at the spot where he disappeared.

The kiss would have meant something to me. What does he mean by that? I thought the whole reason we stopped the kiss was because it could never mean anything to him.

"What was that all about?" Eric asks, sitting.

I blink out of my stupor and look at him, annoyance bristling through me in a flash. I don't want to be sitting with him. I want to be sitting with the person who just vacated his chair.

"I don't know," I concede, feeling guilty for being so unfair. "He came to give me company."

"It looked pretty intense."

It *was* intense.

My eyes drift over Eric's shoulder, but wherever Adrian disappeared, he hasn't returned.

The kiss would have meant something to me.

Why would Adrian say that? Does he really mean it? Better yet, why say it now rather than earlier? Why wait for the moment to pass?

Unless—

My eyes widen when I remember what he'd said to me last night in the woods, right after I'd stopped the kiss. *And it wouldn't mean anything with me.* Not *to* me but *with* me. Maybe the whole reason he said that—and why he'd turned so indifferent afterwards—isn't because he was agreeing that it'd mean nothing to him, but because he thought it'd mean nothing to *me*. And I'd stupidly agreed!

"I'm really sorry," I say to Eric as I scramble out of my chair. "Please excuse me."

"Where are you going?"

I give him another apologetic look as I race to where Adrian disappeared.

There is a huge chance that I've come to the wrong conclusion and that I'm making a mistake in doing this. A *huge* chance. But...Adrian gives me butterflies. He makes me *feel*. Why do I keep making excuses not to move on? Why do I insist on remaining frozen when the world goes on without me? When *he* goes on without me? I never thought I'd experience these feelings for anyone again. Yet here I am, feeling breathless just at the mere thought of Adrian looking at me. And while it's equally as terrifying as it is a huge risk, I don't want to be the girl I was several days ago, holding onto something that's no longer there.

This. This is what's real. This is tangible and exhilarating and *real*. Maybe nothing will come from it. Maybe I will get hurt again. But isn't it better knowing than living beneath *what-if*'s? Isn't it worth the try?

I spot Adrian just as he disappears into the men's room. My heart jumps at the sight of his dirty blonde, tousled hair and the suit that looks far too good on him. When was the last time my heart jumped like this for someone? I know the answer. I also know I'd be a fool not to grab onto it.

It takes willpower to wait by the wall and not dive straight in after him. I drum my fingers against the paintwork while I try to keep hold of my courage, but when Adrian leaves the bathroom and almost walks straight past me, my sudden fear almost lets him.

I shake my head. This is not the time for fear.

"Ophelia," Adrian says when I step in front of him. His eyes glance over my head. "What are you doing here?"

"You said it would mean something to you?" I take another step, enjoying the way I've caught him off-guard. "That kissing me would mean something?" It's a second before he nods his head, still looking startled. "Then we should be doing this already." With one last leap of faith, I close the distance between us and press my lips to his, leaning on my tiptoes to reach him. His surprise hasn't yet worn off. He stumbles back, slamming into the wall behind him, but there's no time for me to feel embarrassed. No time for regret. Not when Adrian finds his footing and kisses me back with an intensity that has my heart speeding. I crave more of the kiss even while it's happening. Wrapping my arms around his neck, I pull him closer.

In an effortless spin, Adrian has my back against the wall. His body presses against mine like he wants more of me, too, and it's a weight that I never want to lose. One of his hands runs through my hair as he tilts my head back, tongue sweeping inside my mouth like he's trying to map me out.

The moan that escapes me does something to him. His hips apply more pressure, hands moving to my waist as he tugs me against him, our bodies flush yet not close enough. Heat rises through my bloodstream, burning hot between my thighs. I press harder.

"Ophelia," he says, breaking from the kiss to whisper my name against my ear. He kisses just below my earlobe before moving it back to my lips.

Goosebumps rise across my flesh. I'd say his name back, but I'm too busy claiming his mouth as my own.

Adrian clearly knows what he's doing in the kissing department, but I try not to think about his experience compared with mine. It doesn't matter. All that matters is that he's kissing me now, and this is unlike any kiss I've ever experienced. This is *his* kiss—one that he owns.

It's a kiss that burns, starting as a tiny spark in my heart and flaring to my soul.

When we're both too breathless to continue, we pause, leaning our foreheads against each other. Adrian's chest heaves, his blue eyes piercing a part of me that I didn't think could be touched again. And as our heart rates slowly steady, bells chime in the distance, marking the start of the most spectacular Christmas Eve.

CHAPTER TWELVE

The bells have stopped, but other noises carry over to us—the sounds of drunkards wishing each other a merry Christmas Eve.

The reminder that we aren't alone should probably deter me from being so close to Adrian. As it happens, there's no place I'd rather be than right here, with my forehead pressed against his, the feel of his lips still dancing across my mouth.

I smile contentedly, eyes opening to meet his.

That's when I see something that has my mood flipping as fast as a tossed coin.

No longer looking at me like he wants to kiss me again, Adrian's face is set like stone. A stone that wants to be someplace else, anywhere that's far, far away from here, away from me.

I deflate like a balloon shot from the sky.

"What's wrong?" I ask.

"I'm sorry." Adrian turns his eyes to the floor. "I need to get out of here."

He doesn't provide more explanation than that before he disconnects his body from mine and leaves. I want to call him back, want to shout out his name and demand why he's doing this, but it's like I've transcended into another world, one where I'm merely a spectator, a phantom incapable of reaching out into the world where he lives.

By the time I manage to snap myself back to my senses, Adrian is nowhere to be seen. I walk around the bar, pushing through the bodies that feel part of that other world, somehow here, somehow not, as I try to make sense of what just happened.

But I don't need to make sense of it. I know what happened. Adrian kissed me, and once it was over, he regretted it.

Maybe he realised it didn't mean anything to him after all.

I don't know how much time passes before my brother finds me. He has that drunken smile on his face, a smile I try to return, but even faking one is a mountain I can't seem to climb.

Thankfully, Jordan is too far gone to register my mood change. I resist the urge to spill it all out to him.

The need to get a second opinion sits heavy on my chest, but what use will that be? He'll tell me what I already know—Adrian regretted it. And then he'll tell me what Evie already tried to—Adrian is a bad person to fall for.

When Jordan drags me to the dancefloor, I don't resist, even though it's the last place I want to be. Evie is there, dancing to a rhythm of her own, and when she sees me, I wonder if I'm doing a very good job at masking my misery because she doesn't say anything about my mood, either.

"Have you seen Adrian?" I ask.

Evie doesn't pause her dancing to answer me. "Adrian? Last time I saw him, he was with Molly."

Her words are like the closing of a coffin. They snuff the air from me. "When did you see that?" I try to keep my breathing steady, but what if he found her after our kiss? Realised he preferred hers to mine?

She shrugs. "I don't know. Can't remember. Why?"

My heart rate continues to increase. Would Adrian really have gone home with Molly? *No.* The word sounds fiercely, followed by a conviction that Adrian wouldn't do that to me. He wouldn't. Something else has to be at play here.

I force myself to relax as the night continues around me, even when Adrian doesn't return. Even as I remain part of that other world.

"He probably had enough of all this and went back to the lodge," Evie says when she finally notices his continued absence. I wish I felt comforted by her lack of concern, but all her words do is inject me with a shot of anxiety. I think of Adrian walking through the woods, drunk and alone, navigating the dark with a hazy brain. What if something terrible has happened to him? What if he's gotten lost because he's too drunk to remember the way?

I approach the subject of leaving with the other two, but it's another half hour before they agree to come with me. The entire walk home, I keep two eyes peeled for Adrian, fear gripping me at every turn. Images of his fallen body, twisted and injured amongst the roots, continue to invade my brain.

"How drunk are you, Phi?" Jordan calls as I rail slightly off track.

"I'm—" Concentration broken, I cut off from telling my brother that I'm now completely sober, yelping instead as my toe stubs a rock. I tumble forward, hands slamming onto the earth in front of me.

The other two laugh, causing my temper to flare, but it lasts only a second before it quickly settles into a dark sense of sadness.

How did tonight end up going so wrong?

The lodge is dark when we get to it. No light through

the windows. The only thing that comforts me is spotting Adrian's shoes and jacket tossed carelessly on the floor.

The breath wooshes out of me when I realise that he's alright. Suddenly exhausted, I leave Jordan and Evie to their continued drinks and patter down the hall, pausing briefly outside Adrian's door. I hesitate before twisting the handle—carefully—and opening the door just enough to see inside. Adrian is lying beneath his quilt with his back to me. Seeing him there slices me in more ways than one. First, there's my intense relief at seeing him here, safe. But there's also a hurt that starts in my chest and claws its way deeper because why did he leave without me?

The anger comes next, sharp and red-hot. Because who the hell kisses someone and then walks away without explanation?

The anger is what sticks around long after I'm buried beneath my own quilt. The anger is what keeps me awake all night, tossing and turning and silently seething. I replay the moment when I noticed the change in his expression—when the regret came hurtling home, and he chose to walk away from me.

Sadness crashes in on me as sudden and sure as the wind outside my window. It smothers the anger like coal over a fire. I curl my knees to my chest, wrapping my arms around them.

If somebody wanted to cut my heart from me this second, I'd let them. Because I don't want to feel this way. Not again. Rejected—*again*. Hurt—*again*. *Rejected. Rejected. Rejected.*

No.

I take a deep breath in, count *one, two, three*, before exhaling with another *one, two, three.*

I am not the girl I was a year ago. I will not break again. I will not let this or anything or anyone ruin the progress that I've made. I've experienced more pain this past year than I have tonight, and I got myself through that.

I will get through this, too.

*

The next afternoon, it's Jordan who raises his concern over Adrian. "Shouldn't we at least ask him if he wants to join us?" he questions. "He hasn't been out of his room all day."

"Okay," Evie concedes. "I'll go ask him." She gets to her feet. I don't want to watch as she marches to Adrian's door, knocking loudly on it, but I do. I watch every second. "Hey," she calls. "We're going out for food. Want to join us? Adrian?" Her knuckles tap the wood again before she looks over at us. "I don't think he's in here."

"Why don't you check?" Again, it's Jordan who says the words, but they may as well come from me.

Evie opens the door enough to peek inside. "He isn't in here," she confirms, flinging it open fully.

Her words crash into me like a wrecking ball, reminding me that no matter how much strength I can muster, it is always a fight to keep the hurt at bay.

As we leave the lodge, the cold air stings my eyes, making them water. At least I hope it's the cold. But Adrian leaving without a word is another reminder that he did the exact same thing after the kiss, and I can't help but wonder if he regrets it so much that he has to be away from me. I wish he was willing to talk it out. I wish he had the courage to say he regrets it to my face. But just leaving like this...

I shake my head as I try to cling to the strength I'd found last night. But I can't deny the hurt I feel, and sometimes strength doesn't equal the absence of pain. Sometimes strength is getting through the day with pain as your companion.

We go for dinner at a restaurant in town. While there, we revisit some of the shops we went into the first time. After the candle store, we walk into the one with the cluttered shelves and unique items. There's a second when my chest tightens as I picture Adrian standing by the grandfather clock cabinet, smirking at me. I walk over to it, searching for something…something…

I find it. There's only one forty-pound pen inside the cabinet, so it has to be the one that Adrian apparently looks at every year he comes here. It sits on a bed of red velvet carved with leaves and twisted vines that wrap delicately around a quartz crystal on top. Beautiful. Maybe even justifiably forty pounds beautiful. I hold the box in my fingers on instinct, then, following that same impulse, I take it to the check-out, carefully storing it in my bag with no clue what do to with it.

It's not like I can give it to Adrian when he refuses to be around me.

"He's still not back," Evie says when we return to the lodge, checking Adrian's room before she does anything else. "Maybe he's gone to the village."

I take the pen to my room and place a bow on top of the box. One way or another, he'll get it for Christmas.

"Shouldn't we check that he's okay?" Jordan is saying when I rejoin them by the TV. "We haven't seen him at all today. Come to think of it, we haven't seen him since last night. What if he's, I don't know, been kidnapped or something?"

Thorns twist in my stomach, but I ignore the feeling as I pull a glass from the cupboard and pour myself a gin.

"I wouldn't worry about that," Evie says, sounding much calmer than I feel. "If anyone tried to kidnap

Adrian, he'd put them on the floor. Besides, he's always like this on Christmas Eve. I'll be surprised if we see him before tomo—"

The glass in my hand crashes on the counter, shattering into tiny shards that shoot off in all directions. Liquid pools on the surface, dripping on the floor and soaking my socks.

"Phi, what the—"

Whatever my brother says next goes unheard. My ears ring with the memory of last night, pinging back to another memory, one I'm certain links to the first.

Adrian, kissing me.

Whispering my name.

Leaning his forehead against mine.

The look in his eyes telling me he wants to do it again.

The look that changes after the bells mark the start of Christmas Eve.

And then the second memory— "Today is the anniversary of your mum's death." I scrunch my eyes closed as everything suddenly makes sense. I don't know how I didn't realise it earlier. How I could be so self-absorbed to not remember.

This is why Adrian isn't here. It isn't because of the kiss we shared. It isn't anything to do with me.

It's because he's in pain.

"Yeah," Evie confirms. "Adrian always spends this day

by himself. I've tried to be there for him before, but he doesn't want it. Ophelia, are you alright?"

"Do you know where he might be?" The guilt is making it difficult to breathe. It squeezes against my ribcage, tighter and tighter until I need to lean against the counter just to maintain balance.

I should have remembered it. I shouldn't have been so wrapped up in my own anguish to not realise the extent of his.

"I don't know." Evie touches my hand. "He always takes himself off on this day. But he always comes back. Really, he'll be fine."

I want so desperately to believe her. But it isn't enough to just stand here and wait. I need to see it with my own eyes.

"Are *you* okay?" Jordan asks, stepping by Evie's side and placing his hand on her shoulder.

"I'm fine. Truly. Today doesn't affect me like it does him."

"Shouldn't we go find him?" I choke.

She gives my hand a squeeze. "That's really nice of you, but he'd honestly prefer it if we didn't. He likes to process his grief alone." Gently nudging me to the side, she starts mopping up the spilt liquid, Jordan working beside her.

"Does your hand sting?" he asks as he picks up broken

shards from the counter.

I look down, noticing the shallow cut crusting with blood just above my index finger. "It does now," I wince. Moving to the sink, I run the cut beneath cold water, watching as red joins in with the stream. "Are you sure you don't know where he could have gone?" I ask quietly.

"Not a clue. I tried to find him once, but it got too dark to continue. He could be in the woods for all I know."

A shiver runs down my spine. Again, the image of Adrian injured and twisted amongst the roots somewhere invades my thoughts.

Tossing sodden paper towels into the bin, Evie turns to me and says, "Phi, I know my brother better than anyone. The best thing we can do for him is leave him alone."

I nod, but the knife twisting in my gut tells me I don't believe her.

Because I'm exactly like Adrian. When I'm in pain or grieving, I like to deal with it on my own. I prefer taking myself to a place where no one can see me, where I can weep into my sheets and face the torment in my head like a one-man battle against thousands.

But I also know that those nights when Jordan came to see me—those nights when he'd perch on the edge of my bed in silence, saying nothing but a thousand things at once—those were the most comforting.

They were comforting because I knew I didn't have to say anything to him. I didn't need to explain how I was feeling for him to understand. He didn't need to understand. He just needed to be there, and it made me feel less alone.

Nobody should grieve alone.

I join Jordan and Evie at the table, a plan forming in my head. When enough time has passed for them not to immediately clock on to what I'm doing, I stand and say, "Does anybody want anything from the store? I'm craving snacks."

"Chocolate, please." Evie doesn't look up from her stack of cards. "Just let me know how much it costs."

"No problem." Wrapping myself up in my coat and scarf, I remember to grab a torch before I leave.

A few steps down the porch is all it takes for me to stop still. It is scarily dark out here. More so knowing that I'm out here alone. My torch hardly pierces into the night, and I don't know if I should aim it at the ground or directly in front of me.

Pushing my fear aside, I focus on what's important: Adrian. And since finding him involves moving, I have no choice but to put one foot in front of the other.

I don't find him at the park centre. He isn't in the bar or the café or the shop. Something tells me not to be surprised. Wherever he is, I don't think it will be easy to find.

Tucking my neck into the wool of my scarf, I rub my fingers together. They're freezing even inside the thick fabric of my gloves.

Where could he be? Anywhere, I realise. He could be anywhere.

Moving again, I exhaust every place I can think of before realising I'll probably never find him. Maybe he's gone into town and is sitting warm at a bar somewhere, oblivious to the fool I'm making of myself out here. Or maybe he's back at the lodge already, laughing with Jordan and Evie at my over-concern.

Disheartened, I turn to go back, torch lighting up a signpost that has me stopping in my tracks. How did I not think of this before? Isn't this the place that Adrian told me about himself—the one he used to visit every year with his mum? His favourite place?

This, I know with a certainty that sits in my gut—this is where he'll be.

CHAPTER THIRTEEN

My heart speeds into a gallop as I head towards the darkest area I've ever seen. Fear digs its claws in me the closer I get. There's a reason this is called the Dark Zone—a place for stargazers. No light interrupts here, and when I dare to look up, the stars shine so bright that I'm momentarily awed.

But I have to keep moving. And the further into the dark I go, the greater my fear becomes. Irrationality takes over. I imagine monsters lurking nearby, shielded by the night, waiting for just the right moment to grab me and pull me into harm.

"Adrian?" I call, too afraid to keep my voice from trembling. My hands shake at the returning silence. "Adrian?" I try again.

Nothing.

There is nothing out here but me and a silence broken only by my own unsteady breathing.

In *one, two, three,* out *one, two, three.*

When I was a little kid, I got trapped in the backroom during a blackout. I felt like the walls were pressing in on me with no air and no way out. Experts will probably claim it's the origins story of my decades-long fear of the dark. Except this is so much worse than back then. This time, I don't have my dad trying to yank the door open or my mum whispering soothing words to me through the wood.

I scrunch my eyes closed as my fear steadily turns into panic.

You need to breathe, I tell myself. *You don't need anyone to help you. You just need you, and you just need to breathe.*

Adrian is out here somewhere—alone—just like me. My gut is telling me to believe it. *He's* the one who needs help right now. And I'm never going to find him if I remain stranded here, paralysed by fear.

Forcing my feet forward, I raise my torch high and plunge deeper into the darkness. With each trembling step, I remind myself that Adrian is grieving, and there's nothing more fearful than that.

"Adrian?" I continue to call. "Adrian? A—" I stop calling when I see a dim light illuminating the grass not far away from me. My fear falls to ash at my feet as

I race towards it, finding Adrian sitting there with his head lowered, empty beer bottles scattered like broken dreams on the grass by his side.

The ache I feel is so potent that I almost crumble. Finding strength, I crouch, placing my hand over his and startling at how cold he feels even through my gloves.

"You're freezing." Shoving my coat off, I wrap it around his shoulders, concern gripping me when he doesn't register that I've done it. Or even that I'm here. "Adrian?"

Finally, he looks up at me, eyes bloodshot and puffy. "Ophelia?"

I point the torch to the side to protect his eyes. "Yes. I'm here."

He stares at me for an unfathomable length of time before doing something that surprises me. Diving forward, he wraps his arms around me with a sob that shatters my heart.

I stroke my fingers through the back of his hair. "Shhh," I soothe. "It's okay."

"I miss her," he sobs, cracking another part of me. But even if I'm battered and bruised by the end of this, barely bone, I'll still stay by his side.

"I know." I stroke his hair again, holding back a sob of my own. All I want to do right now is make this easier for him. Make him okay. But he doesn't need to be okay. He just needs to not be alone. These sobs...They aren't a weakness. They're his way of getting through the pain, of commemorating his mum, and I can't think of anything stronger. "I know," I say again, pulling him closer.

It's a while before the sobs subside and Adrian stills against me. After a moment of quiet, he pulls away, turning his face to the side.

Giving him his moment, I look up at the sky, imagining Adrian's mum watching down on him, a star shining its brightest on the day he needs it most. I imagine her yearning to reach out and comfort him, her son in pain, but never being able to.

Looking down at the boy with his face turned away, I picture him coming here year after year, crouched over, silently weeping, bearing his anguish alone.

It's okay, I think to the sky. *He has me now, and I won't let him be alone on this day again.*

Wrapping my arms around Adrian's shoulders, I pull him close and whisper, "You aren't alone anymore, Adrian. I'm here, and I'm not leaving you."

Every Christmas Eve from now, I know I'll think of him. For that reason, he's claimed a permanent place in me.

"I miss her," he chokes, voice trembling into another

sob. "I miss her so much, Ophelia."

"I know." I place my hand on the top of his hair as I hold him tighter. "I know."

I don't know how long we stay embracing, but eventually, I feel the storm pass through his body as his muscles relax and his breathing evens.

"You feel cold," he says, pulling away from me with a frown like *I'm* the one to be concerned about. He runs his eyes over my body. "Where's your coat?"

A soft laugh escapes me. "You're wearing it."

He looks at the coat wrapped around his shoulders like he's never seen one before. Then, with quick movements that bring pressure to my stomach like building adrenaline, he takes it off his shoulders and wraps it over mine, layering his jacket on top.

Keeping his hands on my shoulders, he asks, "What time is it?"

"Late." Thinking that he needs more than that, I add, "Late enough that Evie and Jordan have probably sent out a search party for me. I told them I was going to the store over an hour ago."

"Don't they know you came to look for me?"

"I didn't tell them."

He drops his hands, faint lines of disapproval crackling along his forehead. "You came out here on your own without telling anyone where you were going?"

"You did the same."

He drops his head with a sigh. "Wait a second." He looks back up, eyes suddenly wide. "You came out here on your own? *You* came out *here*?"

"Yeah?" He's saying it like I've managed to break through a top security prison. "I mean—obviously?"

Picking up my torch, he places it gently in my hands. "Come on. It's too cold out here."

I want to tell him that he's one to talk, considering he was out here for hours before I came along, but when he takes hold of my free hand, all words abort me.

"You didn't get attacked by wild deer?" he asks as we walk.

I keep my eyes on the ground, feeling his hand as if it's an electric wire thrumming with power. "No. But I did think monsters were out here at one point. It was pretty terrifying."

I can hear the laugh in his voice. "You were brave coming out here alone. Especially when you're supposedly scared of the dark."

"I am scared of the dark."

"Then why did you do it?"

"For you." As my words hang like a confession in the air, the hand holding mine becomes almost unbearable—like it's somehow linked to my heart, pumping fuel to make it beat faster.

Adrian moves his thumb across my fingers in soothing strokes, and it's all I can do to keep my heart from bursting out of my chest.

When he stops still with a sudden gasp, I stop with him, heart pounding for a different reason.

But it isn't a monster that's in front of us. It's something that makes my fear scatter for awe to take its place.

Not far from where we stand, a family of deer trot slowly across the clearing, blissfully unaware of our presence.

"They're so beautiful," I whisper as a tiny fawn walks into my torches stream of light. "They aren't scary at all." I look up at Adrian with a smile, finding him watching me with a quiet one of his own.

That's when I realise how close we've gotten—and how I'm clinging to his arm like he's a rope that will pull me to safety.

"I think your phone is buzzing," he whispers.

Feeling the vibration against my side, I pull it out, seeing multiple missed calls from Evie. "Crap. I should probably answer her." I twist away from Adrian as I hit the green button. "Hello?"

"Ophelia?" I hear the panic in her voice and cringe. "Ophelia, where are you? Why didn't you come back?"

"I'm so, so sorry. I'm on my way back now. I bumped into Adrian and—"

"*She bumped into who?*" I hear Jordan ask in the background.

"*Adrian,*" Evie tells him before returning to me. "Where did you find him?"

The way she says it makes me think she doesn't believe it was accidental. "He—he was out for a walk," I lie.

"I'm going for a beer," Jordan says. Then, into the phone, "I hope you know you scared me half to death there, Phi. I thought you'd gone missing."

"I'm sorry."

"Is Adrian okay?" Evie asks.

I glance at him. "He's fine. He's coming back to the lodge with me."

"Jordan wants to go for a beer. Why don't you both come join us?"

Another glance at Adrian tells me going for a beer is the last thing he wants to do. "We're alright. You two enjoy yourselves." I hang up, sliding my phone back into my pocket as I face Adrian. "That was Evie."

"I gathered." He stuffs his hands into the pocket of his hoodie. "You don't want to go for a drink?"

"I'd rather stay with you. If that's alright."

"Do *I* not want to go for a drink?"

I tilt my head. "I don't know. Do you?"

He smirks. "Absolutely not."

We return to an empty lodge. Although it's warmer inside than it is out, I feel a sharp chill—the kind that digs into your bones and settles there.

"I need to get out of these clothes," I say with a shiver.

"If I'd have known that was the reason you wanted to come back..." Adrian trails off, giving me a suggestive look as I pass him his jacket.

Grateful that he's once again capable of humour, I return the look with a raised brow. "I'm getting my pyjamas on. Don't follow me."

It's only when I'm stripping out of my clothes that I realise the kiss last night had *meant* something to him. That he'd wanted for it to happen, and it was only the circumstances that came afterwards that made him leave.

I tug my pyjama pants over my ankles, thoughts whirring. If the kiss had meant something to him, what does that mean for us? Is now the time to ask? No, I realise as I shove a fluffy jumper over my head. Now is the time to let him grieve for his mum and make sure he isn't doing it alone.

He's in the bathroom when I leave my room. With the door left wide open, I see him brushing his teeth inside, eyeing me through the mirror. Wordlessly, I walk to his side, picking up my toothbrush and holding it beneath the water. He doesn't say anything as I begin brushing my teeth, the electric whir of our brushes the only sound. There's something so simplistic about it—so domestic—that I start to think it should feel wrong. But it doesn't. It feels...like I'm standing beside someone I could do this with more often.

I spit. Adrian does the same, eyeing me in the mirror as he wipes his mouth.

"You look tired," he says.

"So do you."

He smiles. "I *am* tired. If I don't go to bed this second, I think I might fall asleep where I'm stood."

Squashing my disappointment that he won't be staying up for longer, I say, "Then you better get yourself to bed."

In the hallway, he pauses at his door. "What are you doing now?"

"Making myself a hot water bottle and going to bed myself."

He seems to debate something. "Could you—could you make one for me, too?"

Knowing I only brought the one with me, I still say, "Sure."

A few minutes later, I enter his room with the water bottle in hand. He's lying on his back, one hand resting behind his head, watching wordlessly as I lay the bottle beside him.

I turn to leave, but he catches my hand.

Butterflies strike my stomach. They rise to my chest, taking the breath from me. Slowly, I turn my head to look at him.

Although he doesn't say anything, his eyes say it for him—a silent plea for me to stay. His eyes dart to something on the wall behind me, and when I turn, I notice a clock hung above a set of drawers, showing twenty minutes until midnight.

Twenty minutes until the worst day of his life is over.

I meet his eyes once more, reading the unspoken question. *Will you stay with me until this is all over?* I answer by closing the door. Adrian moves to the side, giving me space to lie down. I do so, turning my body so that it faces his.

With a breath for courage, I slide my fingers along the quilt, stopping when I reach his hand.

I take hold of it.

A shudder runs through Adrian. He closes his eyes, exhaling as I run my fingers across the back of his.

When his eyes open again, they move downward, a sudden frown appearing as they stop on our hands. He takes mine in his, lifting it with a tilt of his head. "What happened here?" His thumb strokes over the cut

I'd made earlier when I'd dropped the glass. Then there's the graze marks left from when I'd fallen over.

"I've acquired some injuries since the last time we saw each other," I say. His frown deepens. "They don't hurt," I assure him.

He pulls my hand to his chest and closes his eyes again. I close mine. I stop counting the time, but when Adrian releases a deep breath, I know it must be over. Midnight has arrived to take the day away.

When I look at him, I can already see the change on his face. There's a relief there—and an overwhelming tiredness.

"How do you do it?" he asks in a shaky whisper.

"Do what?"

"Open yourself up to a new love when a previous one hurt you. How is it something you want? How—how does the pain not put you off?"

I nestle deeper into the pillow. "Because I think it's worth it." The answer comes easily. "The feeling of falling in love—of loving and being loved—the pain doesn't compare to it. And while it hurts when you lose it, never loving again seems worse to me than never hurting again."

With a small crease between his brows, he plays with my fingers, eyes on them instead of me. "You make it sound so easy."

"Easy?" I laugh at the ludicrousness of it. "*Easy* is the opposite of what it's been for me. It's been a battle. And not just a day-to-day one, either, but a second-by-second one. Accepting that my first love is moving on and now has this life without me...that's been the hardest thing I've ever had to do."

He strokes his thumb over my knuckles. "You loved him."

"I love him."

"And you're too afraid of letting him go."

I'd thought that. For so long, I was afraid of having him as a memory instead of a moment, a last page instead of an ongoing story. I thought I'd never be able to love anyone other than him or imagine a future without him by my side. But now...I look at Adrian's hand stroking mine and wonder if I might be able to love someone else.

Could I love this tortured boy in front of me? It feels like it might be easy.

"I'm not afraid."

The stroking stops. His eyes flick up to meet mine. "But you said you still love him."

"I will always love him. Breaking up with someone doesn't change that. All it does is change the way you direct it."

He takes a few breaths. "He was a fool to let you go."

And you? I want to ask. *Would you ever take hold?*

His eyes are so tired. Tired and puffy. A sign that he's been crying today and a reminder that now isn't the time to pressure him. It's the time to be his friend.

I change the subject. "What's your favourite movie?"

His brows flick up, but he doesn't question my sudden change in topic. "The Lord of the Rings," he answers.

My surprise is genuine. "Really?"

"Yes. And don't you dare make fun of me for it."

"I would never!" To show him that I'm a fan, too, I do my best Gollum impression, causing him to stare at me in shock.

"You're a fan?" he asks.

"Of course. The Two Towers is my favourite, but I like them all."

He laughs beneath his breath. "Your Gollum impression was scarily good, by the way. You're such a nerd for doing that."

I pinch his arm. "I'll take that as a compliment."

"What's your favourite genre of music?"

"Can't choose. Wait, no—I can. It's Taylor Swift."

"That isn't a genre."

"She's a genre in herself, and don't you dare argue with me on it." I smile as he rolls his eyes. "What's yours?"

"Alternative."

"I can see that. Your biggest fear?"

"Falling in love."

His answer surprises both of us. I can see the shock in his eyes, and I wonder if it's something he's ever confessed aloud before or even to himself.

And as the words resonate, the ache in my chest grows to a point where it goes beyond physical.

Pulling his hand toward me, I whisper, "Don't be afraid of falling in love, Adrian. The landing is better than you can imagine."

CHAPTER FOURTEEN

I open my eyes to the dim light of morning.

For a second, I'm disoriented.

This isn't my room.

As my eyes strain to take in the details, memories of the night before return to me in flashes. I see Adrian with his head bent forward, his body cold and alone. I feel his sobs as he wraps his arms around me, see his tired and puffy eyes as they strain to stay awake. I watch as he falls asleep by my side, exhausted after confessing his biggest fear.

His fear of falling in love.

He's still asleep now. Still by my side with his fingers lying loosely beside mine. He'd held on to my hand until the depths of slumber forced him to release me.

Adrian is different in the morning. Vulnerable. His face is relaxed, peaceful in sleep, and I resist the urge to reach out and brush his hair away from his forehead or run my fingers across his long eyelashes.

With a quiet sigh, I try to imagine what his life has been like for these past several years. A life void of love—living day by day with a guard up—must be lonely and exhausting.

He loves his sister. I know that much is true. But he loved her before what happened to their mum, and I don't think he's allowed himself to experience new love ever since.

This beautiful man. This ferocious, sincere, surprisingly gentle man. Yes—he would be easy to love. But will he ever have the courage to love in return?

"It's Christmas!" Evie's voice sounds like an alarm throughout the lodge, bouncing off the walls and landing on top of us. "It's Christmas, it's Christmas, it's Christmas!"

Adrian's eyes begin slowly opening. It looks like he's awakening from the deepest of sleep, and if I could, I'd make it so he could rest for longer.

"Morning," he smiles, voice croaky and adorable from hours of unuse.

The smile makes my stomach dip. "Morning," I whisper back.

His smile deepens as he closes his eyes again. I wonder if it's his sleepiness that's keeping his guard lowered because part of me expected him to shove me from the bed. For a second, I imagine myself staying here all day, just watching him.

I think that would be easy, too.

"Adrian," Evie says from outside his door, "have you seen Ophelia? She isn't in her room."

I hear her fingers on the handle, and in a flash of panic, I dive to the other side of the bed approximately one second before Evie opens his bedroom door. I land with a painful thud, rolling as close to the wooden frame as possible.

"Can't you knock?" Adrian reprimands his sister. "I could have been naked."

"Have you seen Ophelia?"

"Do I look like I've seen Ophelia?"

Evie is silent for a moment. "You need to work on your cheery voice in a morning. It's Christmas!"

When the door closes, I wait a few seconds before poking my head up.

"Yeah, she's gone." Adrian chuckles at the sight of me before stretching his long arms to yank me back upright.

I rub my knee, the one I hit the hardest, already regretting the force with which I launched myself from the bed.

"Are you alright?" His brows furrow as he looks at the

hand rubbing my knee.

"I'm fine. Just landed a little hard is all."

"You know you didn't need to hide, right? It's not like we were doing anything." Swinging his legs from the bed, he bends forward, pulling my pyjama leg up to my knee to examine the damage.

I try to keep my breathing steady as one hand cups the back of my calf. "You wouldn't have minded Evie seeing me in here?"

"No." He touches the tender area—where I already predict there'll be a bruise—as I try not to react to his answer or his touch.

"She would have asked questions about us."

"And I would have given her the answers."

My heart decides that it wants to start risking itself again. "And what would that have been?"

"That we're—" He cuts himself off, hand stilling as he looks up at me. After a few seconds, he clears his throat, looking at my leg again. "Your knee seems fine, but I'd hold off from sustaining any more injuries. You look like the embodiment of a battlefield."

"I feel like one." Those aren't the words I wanted to say. What I wanted was to ask him what he thinks we are, but I can already see his guard getting built back up, brick by brick, exiling me to the outskirts where he keeps everyone else.

Just when I think he's sealed himself off completely, he brushes his thumb over another bruise, one just below my knee, and lowers my pant leg with a gentleness that shatters an ache in me. He keeps his hand by my ankle, looking up again.

This feeling—the clenching and swooping of my stomach—*this* is what I've been missing. It's like a thousand fireworks releasing into a clear night sky, overpowering and beautiful and completely breathtaking.

"I'll just call her," I hear Evie say. It takes me a few seconds to register what she means, and when I do, I'm back to launching myself across the bed to grab my phone from beneath the pillow I used. I switch it to silent just in time for it not to be heard as her name flashes across my screen.

Adrian rolls his eyes as I smile back at him. "I'll go lure Evie into the living room," he says as he approaches his door. "You should go to the bathroom and come up with an excuse as to why you couldn't hear her." His hand stills on the handle. He turns, looking straight at me. "And thank you. For last night, I mean."

He's gone before I can get the words *you're welcome* through the shock he's made me feel.

Once I know the coast is clear, I sneak into the hall, quickly shutting myself into the bathroom. At the sink, I splash cold water over my face and allow myself to imagine having Adrian by my side again, doing something so simplistic as brushing his teeth. If I could, I'd relive that part of last night for a second, maybe third time.

I don't look at Adrian as I enter the main room. I know if I do, I'll give my growing feelings away, and I'm still unsure what he thinks about me.

"You're here," Evie says, clearly confused.

"I'm here," I confirm.

"But..." She looks over my shoulder. "From where? I've been calling for you."

"Oh. I was in the bathroom. Had my earphones in."

"In the bathroom?"

"I've been listening to an audiobook." Thankfully, I'm enough of a book fiend for that to be just about believable, but a cough from Adrian tells me he thinks I could have done better with my excuse.

"It's Christmas morning," Evie continues. "Why am I the only one who seems excited?"

"I'm excited by that smell." I turn to face the kitchen, where Jordan has an apron wrapped around his waist and a spoon in his hands. Out of the two of us, he's undoubtedly the better cook. He finds the practice of it therapeutic, whereas I find standing by a stove, trying to time things just right, completely stress-inducing.

"Need a hand?" I ask.

"I've got it all under control, thanks."

Happy to be of no use in the kitchen, I join Evie on the sofa, allowing myself one quick glance at Adrian and feeling a thrill to find him staring straight at me.

"Can we open the presents yet?" Evie asks, twisting to face Jordan, who wipes his hands on his apron.

"Just let me prep the veg, and I'll be free to join you."

The present exchange is basically Adrian and I sitting around while Jordan and Evie pass presents to one another—I got them a ticket to an amusement park since I know they both love rollercoasters, and they got me a set of silk pyjamas. It's nice to watch, but it reminds me of last year and all the years before that when I was spoilt by my second family. I allow myself a moment to wonder about them. Have they finally managed to get out for dinner like they always talked about? Or are they at home, all nine of them huddled around the table as the dishes pile high? Then I'm back in the room, watching the glee on Evie's face as she opens the necklace Jordan spent a fortune on, and I'm listening to Jordan's laughter. Jordan, who hasn't been spoilt at Christmas since he was a child.

I tuck my knees to my chin with a smile. Yes, this year is nothing like I imagined it would be, but it's also lovelier than I could have hoped for.

"Who's this for?" Evie flips a small, thin parcel over in her hands. "It doesn't have a name on it."

Recognising it as the pen I bought at the store while searching for Adrian yesterday—the one I bought *for* him—I sit upright, my face heating.

I'd forgotten I'd put it under there. If I'd been thinking clearly, I would have held back, giving it to him in private. Now I have to admit to what I've done in front of everyone.

"Anybody want to claim it?" Evie holds it out to us as though she's happy to take it for herself if nobody else does. "Someone here had to have put it there."

I turn my face to Adrian and force out, "It's for you."

"For me?" His eyes widen. "You got me a gift?"

My face heats like a thermostat turned high. "Call it even for the mochi."

As Adrian takes the present from Evie, I resist the urge to slam my eyes closed. The cringe is about two seconds away from showing on my face. I stare at the fireplace instead, incapable of watching his reaction. What if he doesn't like it? Worse, what if he pretends to like it when everyone can clearly see the hate on his face?

"Oh my God." The words come from Evie. Eyes darting to her face, I find her looking at her brother with an expression I can't make out.

Braving it, I turn my eyes on Adrian and, with a quiet gasp, realise that he has tears in his eyes. He wipes them away, putting the pen back in the box with a sniff.

What colossal mistake have I made here?

"I'm so sorry," I quickly say, unsure how to fix this. "I thought you'd like it. I thought—"

My words cut off as his quiet voice reaches me. "I went looking for it. Yesterday." He stares directly at me. "I went into town to buy it, but it had already been sold. What you said bothered me," he adds, looking over at his sister. "About somebody else buying it. So when I saw it was gone, I thought I'd lost it forever." His eyes move to the carpet, brows creasing as he loses himself to the memory of seeing the pen gone for the first time in how many years? He shakes his head, looking at me again. "Thank you. I'm really glad you're the one who bought it."

I hold his eyes, wondering if this is part of the reason why he'd been so upset when I found him yesterday. A yearning to hug the boy who thought the pen was missing almost cripples me, but we're here now, and he has it, and this can still be a good day.

Squeezing his hand, I say, "You're welcome, Adrian."

Jordan clears his throat. Retracting my hand, I busy myself with tidying the wrapping paper.

When I return from taking the paper to the recycling

bin outside, Evie joins me by the kitchen sink. "That was really nice of you," she says as I pour myself a water. "What you did for Adrian. I've never seen him so moved."

I look over at where he's sitting on the sofa. Although he still appears tired, he doesn't seem anywhere near as upset as yesterday. It's like the storm has passed, preparing itself for another year. Is there a way to keep it at bay for good?

"You're doing it," Evie tells me.

I blink away from Adrian. "Doing what?"

"Giving Adrian *The Look*."

Heat blazes up my neck because I think I know what she means. "What look?"

"The look that says you're falling for him." She eyes me for a few seconds longer before turning her attention to her brother, analysing him instead. Tilting her head, she ponders, "I wonder…"

"What?"

She looks back at me. "If he's falling for you, too."

My sharp inhalation goes unnoticed as Jordan calls Evie over to show her something on his phone. Although she gives me a *We'll Continue This Later* look, I'm grateful when she leaves me alone. If we continued this conversation, I'm not sure what I'd say to her.

The truth is, I think I am falling for Adrian. Falling in

a way that happens little by little, step by tentative step, and the further I go, the less scared I feel.

What I've really been fearing is the unknown. Fearing the change. I've been afraid to experience new firsts because it means the last really was the last. The hardest part of any breakup is letting go. There's always a voice in the back of your brain telling you to hold on, to persevere. It whispers that it isn't over yet, that he'll come back. But the truth is, I can't always be waiting. If I keep doing that, if I remain sitting by the window with the lights turned on, I'll be freezing myself in time, not loving myself enough to move forward. I need to let the candle burn out.

Besides, just because a person leaves your life doesn't mean they weren't worth the time you gave them. It doesn't mean they didn't enrich your life or make it better. Letting go doesn't have to be a sad thing.

"You okay there, Phi?" Jordan asks, looking over at me as Evie leans over his phone.

I give him a small smile. "Just having a moment."

"It looks like a deep moment." His eyes are concerned, but they don't need to be.

"I'm appreciating what I have in front of me," I say, looking at each of them in turn.

Jordan.

Evie.

Adrian.

The latter is who I stay staring at. He smiles back at me in a way that makes me feel understood. Although his experience is different to mine, loving and losing someone has left Adrian frozen in time, too. My only hope is that we can both find a way to move forward—that he can hold the memories of his mum in his heart in a way that's beautiful, not painful.

Maybe we'll both be able to light a new candle. One we won't need to blow out.

Evie moves away from Jordan to scutter past me in the kitchen, pulling four wine glasses from the cupboard. She fills them halfway with the white merlot she'd been saving for today. Handing a glass to each of us, she holds hers high. "To new beginnings," she says.

"To new beginnings," we echo.

After a delicious dinner of turkey and beef and buttery mashed potato with caramelised vegetables on the side—Jordan truly outdid himself—I join Adrian in the kitchen. We're both on cleaning duty since Jordan enlisted Evie's help towards the end of his long slog. I don't complain about it. Not when I can stand by Adrian's side and feel the warmth of his body heating my skin.

"You really suit rubber gloves," I tell him, smirking at the sight of them pulled high up his forearms.

He splashes soapy water at me. "Shut up."

"You know I can do that back, right?" To prove my point, I dip my hand in the water and splash it on his face.

He holds his hands up in a desperate attempt to block my attack. "I didn't think you had the nerve."

I do it again, making him laugh this time.

"Is that Adrian laughing on Christmas day?" Evie calls from where she's lying on the couch, healing from her food hangover. "Who are you, and where are you hiding my brother?"

We clear the dishes away and join the other two by the TV because apparently, neither Jordan nor Evie can stomach getting drunk again. That works for me. There's no other way I'd prefer to spend Christmas evening than beneath a blanket with a movie playing.

With the lights switched off, Evie uses Jordan as a pillow, sprawling across his chest with their quilt tucked up to her chin. I pull my blanket up to my shoulders. Adrian steals some from me, covering his thighs with the soft tartan and raising his brows as if daring me to take it back.

As it happens, I like sharing a blanket with him.

He doesn't seem fazed by the Christmas movie that's been chosen—*A Wonderful Life*—but I still steal glances at him just in case the day gets too overwhelming.

About halfway through the movie, he nudges my arm.

I twist to look at him, fully accepting the thrill that shoots through me when I meet his eyes in the dark. He presses his finger to his lips, nodding over at the other sofa, where I find Evie and Jordan with their eyes closed, clearly sleeping.

I laugh quietly. "I think they've been partying too hard."

"I'd send them to bed, but then I'd have to come up with a reason as to why I'm not moving to the free sofa."

"Why wouldn't you move to the free sofa?"

He doesn't say anything else, but I see the shadow of a smile as he moves his eyes to the TV. My stomach swoops at the thought of him staying here because he's next to me. But if that somehow is the case, I can relate. Even though I'm aching from sitting in the same position for an hour, I wouldn't move from his side if given the option.

"Are you enjoying the movie?" I ask, realising that he's been quiet for a while.

His voice whispers back to me. "I'm not watching the movie."

Swinging my eyes towards him, I find his eyes on the TV. "Then what are you watching?"

He smirks. "Nothing. I'm thinking."

For some reason, that makes me more nervous than if he'd told me he was watching me. I wait for him to elaborate, and when he doesn't, my heart thud, thud, thuds in anticipation. "About?"

He glances at Jordan and Evie before meeting my eyes. Leaning closer, he murmurs, "It wouldn't be appropriate to say aloud."

I swallow. Facing the TV again, I try to follow the movie, but now I'm thinking about other things, too. Things that wouldn't be appropriate to say aloud.

About Adrian.

About the kiss that almost happened and the kiss that finally did.

About what might happen if we were the only two people in here.

I clear my throat. Adrian rolls his shoulders. His hand, the one resting nearest to mine, moves a little closer. Although there's no contact, I can feel those fingers as if their nerve endings are attached to my own, connecting us by something that no one else can see. He moves his hand closer. With a *zing*, our pinkies touch. It's only our pinkies, yet I'd swear a furnace has started burning, heating from the tips of my fingers down to my toes.

With a racing heart, I move my pinkie so that it falls on top of his. He does the same. Slowly, finger by finger, our hands entwine.

We stay like that for the rest of the movie, and when the credits roll in, we don't move.

It's just us and the dark and two ferociously beating hearts.

CHAPTER FIFTEEN

Evie makes a noise that has us both jumping in fright. I pull my hand away from Adrian's as she sits up, disorientated and sleepy, causing Jordan to wake up with her.

"We missed the movie," she yawns, stretching her arms out. "Should we put it on again?"

"Correction," Adrian says, "*you* missed the movie." Beneath the blankets, he reaches for my hand again, taking it from my lap and holding it in his. Amusement drips into his voice as he adds, "Although I wouldn't mind watching it again."

It takes all of my self-control not to react.

"It's a great movie, isn't it?" Jordan says, adding his yawn to Evie's. "But I can't stay awake. I think I need an early night."

"Me too." Evie yawns again. "What about you two?

Are you going to bed or staying up?"

I open my mouth, not knowing exactly what I'm going to say, but Adrian beats me to it.

"I think I'll stay up for a bit." He turns to face me. "Ophelia? Fancy a few games before we call it a night?"

"S—sure." The adrenaline I'd felt when our fingers touched turns into a sudden, ferocious fear. It was one thing *imagining* being alone with him, but to actually *be* alone...

The fear magnifies as Jordan and Evie grab their quilt and slowly make their way to the hallway, shutting us in as they close the door behind them. It's so easy to imagine Adrian and I being the only two in the lodge. The other two could be back home, miles and miles away. I will myself to calm down as another shot of fear enters my bloodstream. I'm excited, not afraid. *Excited*.

Except I know myself well enough to also know that I can't fool myself over how I'm feeling.

So instead, I accept my fear and tell myself that it's okay to feel this way. There's no pressure to do anything. If I say no to Adrian, if I explain how I'm feeling to him, he'll understand. He'd never press for more.

"What game do you want to play?" he asks. I watch as he moves around the table to a stack of board games. Part of me thought he was joking about the games, but as he picks up the top box and waves it at me, I realise this is actually happening.

I pull out a seat at the table. "How about some cards?"

"Cards." He nods, putting the box back and picking up a small pack of decks. "Good choice." As he takes the seat opposite me, I realise that he seems nervous, too. He looks at the table instead of me, his breathing shaky. "Ready to lose?" he asks.

"Ready to whoop your ass." I want to sound playful, but the words come out all clumsy and unsure. There's an awkwardness in the air, one I haven't felt with him before, and even though I want to smother it, I also don't know how.

"Shit." With fumbling fingers, Adrian drops the cards. They sprawl across the table, some landing on the floor.

"I'll help." I crouch down, scraping them together with a heart that wants to escape this lodge and find a haven somewhere else. "*Ouch*," I say as my head thwacks the table on my way back up.

"Are you alright?" Adrian reaches for me, letting his hand hang there without making contact.

"I'm fine," I say, rubbing the sore spot. "I just—" Meeting his eyes, I see the situation for what it is. Adrian —frantic and unsure of himself—and me—red-faced and heart beating double-time.

A laugh bubbles out of me.

Bafflement replaces his concern. "You're laughing?"

"I'm not laughing, I'm—" Another laugh bursts out of me. "I'm sorry. I can't help it."

"What is happening to us?" Adrian runs a hand through his hair with an amused chuckle. "I'm so nervous."

Hearing him admit his nerves to me calms my laughter. "Why are you nervous?"

"Because you—" He stops what he's saying, swallowing the words before trying again. "Because you make me nervous."

In the ensuing silence, we stare at each other. I remember the kiss and how it felt to have his lips pressed against mine. Has he ever been made to feel this way before? Will he want to kiss me again?

Pulling the cards towards me, I tidy them into a neat stack. "For the record," I say, "you make me nervous, too."

"Then I count myself as a lucky man."

My hand stills. While my nerves have returned, they're different this time. They're the kind I don't want to let go of because they only come when you're lucky enough to be excited by someone.

It gets easier after that. The air lightens. There isn't any flirting involved as we play a round of *Go Fish*, but there is laughter, and hearing that sound coming from him on this day is better than any gift that might have been purchased.

"How is it that you keep beating me?" he asks, handing me another card.

"I'd call it a lucky streak, but luck has nothing to do with it."

"You're cocky." Despite his words, he's nodding in approval, his smile stretching wider as he adds, "Or maybe a cheat?"

"Ooft." I shake my head. "The words of a sore loser."

I can tell that neither of us wants to go to bed. Even as the evening stretches into night and the night into early morning. We keep stretching it out. After playing one game, we play another, and once we're done with that game, we pull out another box. It's only when we're both yawning and blinking from exhaustion that the subject of bedtime is broached, and that's only because if we don't move, Jordan and Evie will find us asleep here in the morning.

"I think I need to call it a night," I say.

Adrian stifles another yawn. "Me too."

We leave the table as it is, too tired to clear it, and make our way to the hallway.

I pause at the door, realising something that turns my blood cold. "Tomorrow's our last night here."

Adrian frowns. "You're right."

"We'll be leaving the day after." It's an obvious

statement, but somehow, I hope saying it can make it untrue. I don't want this trip to end.

"We will."

My eyes move towards the kitchen. There's this feeling in my stomach—an intense twisting telling me I shouldn't go to bed yet. That I should stretch this out for longer.

"I think I'll have a glass of water before bed," I say.

I move to the kitchen sink, my heart pounding when I feel the weight of Adrian beside me.

"I think I'll have one, too."

Together, we take small, deliberate sips, watching each other as our glasses barely empty. I pull myself up onto the counter. Adrian stays by the sink. When he's done, he places his empty glass on the side and looks over at me. I take smaller sips, wondering if I can drag this out indefinitely if I never finish the drink.

Eventually, I can't help but finish it. I place my glass next to his and meet his eyes again, fearful that this marks the end. What if tomorrow we don't get another opportunity to be alone? Is this the last time I'll be with him like this?

Adrian is looking at me with words in his eyes. When none of them come, I decide I'll wait here all night until he's ready to say them. I'll wait for as long as it takes, even if I have to hold myself up with pins and pry my eyes open.

He looks to the side, eyes flinging back to me as his mouth opens.

"I'm sorry for the other night," he says. His Adam's apple bobs. "Just in case I don't get a chance to say this again. I'm sorry for kissing you and then rushing out like that. It was a shitty thing to do, and it wasn't fair on you."

My mouth works for a moment. I'm not sure what I expected him to say, but I know it wasn't an apology. "You don't need to be sorry. Really. I understand why you did it. I would have done the same."

"No, you wouldn't." His eyes hold mine like I'm his willing hostage. "You wouldn't have left me like that."

I want to say that yes, I would have, but it's hard saying anything when I'm pinned beneath the intensity of his burning blue gaze.

So instead, I admit a secret. "I don't want to leave you tonight."

Surprise flickers across his face. "Are you still tired?"

"No," I answer. "Are you?"

"Not even a little bit."

Adrenaline awakens me further.

We stare at each other for a beat longer before he takes a slow step towards me. Then another. His last step brings him to my knees, where I'm still perched on the counter.

"You can come closer," I say.

His eyes flash as he steps between my thighs. "You drive me crazy, Ophelia Jones. Did you know that?" He leans closer, hands holding the counter on either side of me, his eyes holding mine as though he expects me to jerk away. When I don't, he presses his lips to mine, tentative at first. Tentative and testing.

Our eyes remain open, questioning one another, but it adds an intimacy to the kiss, and I feel a fire blazing deep within me, burning along the edges of containment.

I almost shatter when I see the tortured look in his eyes as he pulls away.

Like a moth drawn to the fire within me, he comes back, lips pressing to mine again with the tenderest of touches.

He closes his eyes this time.

I close mine.

Whatever test we just put ourselves through, I know we passed it.

Wrapping my arms around his shoulders, I bring him closer. He pulls me by the hips so I'm sitting on the edge of the counter, closest to him. There's an ache in me that can't be soothed by anything else. It needs him. The kiss gets deeper, quicker, fevered, even—like we've forgotten self-preservation, and we're dropping every wall ever built.

I cling to him, pull at his shirt, try to hold on to this moment of searing desire because I haven't felt it in so long, and I don't want it to end.

All too soon, he's pulling away again, holding me at arm's length with a look in his eyes that I'm starting to know well.

"I'm not going anywhere," I assure him, although I can't blame him for fearing I might. Haven't I told him over and over again that I want something with meaning? A kiss is one thing. Taking it further is no small thing for me.

I look deep into Adrian's eyes and know, with absolute certainty, that even if it meant nothing to him, it would still mean something to me. *He* means something to me. I can tell that from the way my heart is racing and from the way it broke after seeing him cry.

And it's enough.

Pulling my jumper over my head, I toss it onto the counter, not shying away as his eyes trail downward. He does the same with his jumper, lifting it over his head and allowing me a moment to savour the bare, toned chest in front of me, all hard muscle, a new territory that I want to explore with my fingers. He leans forward to kiss me again, but at the last second, he looks towards the door, dropping his head with a soft chuckle.

"What is it?" I ask.

Bringing his mouth to my ear, he whispers, "We aren't the only two here."

I slap my hands over my mouth when I remember the existence of my brother and Evie. If either of them saw us like this, I'd be mortified enough to never show my face again.

Adrian places a finger over his lips. With one arm, he lifts me from the counter, using his free hand to collect our clothes.

I wrap myself around him as he carries me into the hallway, opens the door to his bedroom and quietly closes it behind him.

My heart is thudding again.

He lowers me to my feet, taking a shuddering breath. "Are you sure about this?"

In answer, I unbutton my jeans, wriggling my way out of them. They fall quietly to the floor.

Standing in nothing but my underwear, I keep my eyes on his face, watching as his eyes move slowly downward. I've never been body-conscious, but that's because the only person who's ever seen it has always made me feel good about myself. This is different. This is new. Yet somehow…I don't feel afraid.

Adrian's eyes lift to meet mine again. "You're perfect."

I don't miss a beat. "So are you."

He smiles before frowning. "I'm sorry if I do anything wrong. This is all new to me."

New to *him*? How is that possible? Is it because, for the first time, he's nervous about it happening? Or is there something more to it than that?

As he fumbles with the buckle on his belt, I step forward. "Let me help you."

He drops his hands with a chuckle as I take over. "I've never needed help taking my pants off before."

I laugh. "I'm glad to be the first." I crouch as I lower his jeans, pulling them past his knees. When I reach his feet, I look up at him, feeling my heart in my throat as I lean closer, placing a gentle kiss on his inner thigh.

He stares at me for an unfathomable length of time before breathing, "How is it possible that you exist?" With that comment, he kicks his jeans away from his feet and lifts me, dropping me on his bed with a gleam in his eyes.

"Shh," I giggle, pressing my finger to my lips. "We don't want to wake them."

"You know I'd *really* love to hear you make noises that would wake the entire park, but if we have to do this quietly..."

He lowers himself over me, kissing my earlobe before moving to my cheek, my neck, my clavicle. With one hand, he reaches over, switching off the light so we're left with the dim glow of a lamp.

As he pulls his boxers down, a nervous excitement starts in my stomach and flares in my chest.

I'm really doing this.

I really *want* to do this.

After I wriggle out of my underwear, there's a moment when we both just pause, watching each other, almost as if we're waiting for the other to back out.

"You're sure about this?" he murmurs again. In answer, I pull him onto me, feeling the weight of him as our bodies press together.

He scrunches his eyes closed, biting his bottom lip before choking, "One moment." Reaching over me, he fumbles for something, pulling a condom from his wallet. Once it's on, he meets my eyes. "We're really doing this."

"We're really doing this," I confirm, and there isn't a single part of me that's telling me it's wrong.

As he slowly enters me, I raise one hand so that it holds the top of the headboard. The other I use to stifle the moan the feel of him brings out of me.

He dips his head, tracing his fingers up my raised arm until it's holding my hand. With another gentle thrust, he pushes further into me.

Even with his gentleness, the bed thuds against the

wall, making a noise I'd really rather no one else heard. Adrian, seeing the look in my eyes, quickly pulls out of me and stands by the side of the bed. I'm about to protest—about to tell him that if the alternative is stopping altogether, I'd rather risk the noise—but then I realise what he's doing.

Gently pulling me to my feet, he takes the quilt and pillows from the bed and layers them on the floor, guiding me onto them before lowering himself over me again.

There's a moment when he just looks at me, and I look at him.

"I want to do this right," he whispers, brushing my hair from my face. His lips press against mine as he pushes his way inside me again. Which is good since I need his mouth to stifle my moans.

With every kiss comes a thrust that takes him deeper, sending pleasure waves shuddering through me with an ache that can't be contained. I want more of him, I want all of him, I want whatever he's willing to give.

I kiss him back, keeping to his rhythm—my lips crushing against his with every thrust. He breaks away and lowers his head, using my breast to stifle a moan of his own. He kisses my collarbone next, murmuring my name against my skin.

With a gentle touch, I lift his face, wanting

desperately to watch as pleasure takes control of him. I've never seen him look like this before, so vulnerable, tortured, and beautiful. There's a slight sheen on his forehead, and his eyes are hooded, brows drawn together like he's fighting the urge to make noise.

Carefully, I maneuverer us so that he's the one on his back, and I'm sitting on top of him. All the while, he watches me with an expression that makes me feel one-of-a-kind.

Rolling my hips over him, I feel double pleasure when I see his eyes roll into the back of his head. He moans, and I quickly throw my hand over his mouth to stifle the noise. He kisses my palm, kisses my every finger before pulling me towards him and kissing my lips again.

Once he breaks from the kiss, he turns me so that I'm on my side, back towards him. He slides his arm beneath my neck, allowing me to use him as a pillow as he carefully positions himself and enters me from behind. Using his free arm, he wraps it around my waist and tugs me closer.

"It's never felt like this before," he whispers, pressing his lips to the top of my hair.

I turn my face towards him, pressing my lips to his as he moves slower, deeper, reaching parts of me that I never thought could be reached again.

Something blooms in my chest as his tongue glides

against mine. It starts in the middle and spreads to my ribcage, giving me a deep sense that it's never felt like this for me before, either.

This is different.

This is him.

This is something that I don't want to let go of.

CHAPTER SIXTEEN

Adrian

I wake up happy, which isn't something I'm accustomed to feeling first thing in the morning. Especially here, at this place, where I have most of my nightmares.

It takes me a few moments to realise why.

I smile into my pillow, tugging Ophelia closer. I could wake up to the smell of her every morning. Could hold her for days rolling into nights transitioning into mornings.

We're still on the floor. Part of the reason for that is because, after our first round together, I couldn't get enough of her. The sex was unbelievable. So out-of-this-world incredible that it made me wonder why I hadn't had it like that before.

But how could I? She hadn't come along yet.

A finger runs the length of my nose, causing my eyes to fling open. I see Ophelia's face in front of me, nestled close to my neck, wearing a smile that mirrors my own.

"Why are you smiling like that?" she asks.

My smile deepens. "I could ask you the same thing."

"I'm smiling because I'm happy."

Warmth blooms within my chest. I tug her closer, running my finger down her nose as she did with mine and grinning when it makes hers crinkle. "I'm smiling for the same reason."

She takes a deep, contented breath, closing her eyes again.

As I watch her this time, a doubt forms within my chest, settling over my heart in the same way a dark cloud covers a suntrap in shadow. I wonder...was last night a first for the both of us? Did she have meaningless sex for the first time in her life while I experienced the opposite?

I know she said she wanted it to mean something to her—she's said it enough times for my doubt to seem unqualified—but how could I be that lucky? How can I be the one to help her move on? Maybe she finally decided to let loose and have sex just for enjoyment. If that is the case, I can't blame her. Meaningless sex can be fun, wild—and she clearly enjoyed herself last night.

But after experiencing the other side of it, I can't bear the thought of being that person to her. Of being the interlude before she meets someone she can love again.

I take a deep, shuddering breath, causing Ophelia to nestle closer.

There's that warmth in my chest again. I'm starting to realise it comes whenever I'm near her. It intensifies whenever I'm fortunate enough to feel her touch. And when I think about last night—and how fucking unreal it was—I swear I'm seconds away from bursting into a spontaneous flame.

I've always enjoyed sex. I won't deny that. But the people I've had it with have never known anything past my first name. It's always been for the act of it, the simple pleasure, and never anything more. I've never looked at a woman and felt in complete awe of her before. Never wanted to kiss every inch of her skin or whisper her name as I watched the pleasure on her face because it tripled my own. Never wanted to hold her in my arms the next morning and keep her there for as long as she'll stay.

I've never wanted to protect and heal and be something *more* to her before.

And I definitely haven't been able to imagine myself with only her before.

Ophelia's smile is content, but all too soon, she's

pulling away from me, holding the quilt to her chest as she sits up, covering that perfect body of hers.

"What are you doing?" I ask, sounding needy and pathetic.

"I should shower before the other two wake." With movements too quick for me to stop, she reaches across the floor for her jumper, pulls it over her head and stands.

"Do you have to leave now?" I complain. Seriously, what is wrong with me?

"Yes." She smiles and jumps out of the way as I reach for her. "I don't want a repeat of yesterday when Evie almost caught me."

As she collects her things and turns for the door, I'm hit with a sharp stab of panic that surprises me.

If she leaves now, will I ever be alone with her like this again?

"You don't want them to see us together?"

"Not if—" She cuts herself off, hesitating. "Not if, um, we aren't...anything."

Because she doesn't want us to be anything?

The panic becomes unbearable as she reaches for the handle. Why do I get the sense that if she leaves now, I won't get to hold her again? I'll only get to miss her. "Ophelia, wait—" She turns back. "About last night—" I start. "I know you said you only wanted sex if it's meaningful—but—" Why can't I get my words out? Why can't I say what I need her to hear?

"It's okay," she says with a shake of her head. "You told me from the start that it never means anything to you. I don't expect to be different. It doesn't—" she pauses, colour blooming on her cheeks. "It doesn't change the fact that it meant a lot to me."

She turns away again just as hope enters my heart and stops me from breathing.

I reach for her hand before it can lift for the handle. This time, when she turns to face me, she looks as breathless as I feel. "Last night—" I swallow. My heart is pounding, but I know I'll regret it if I don't say these words to her. "Nothing has ever meant more to me than what happened between us."

Surprise flickers across her face. She looks briefly to the side before her eyes flick back to me. "It meant something to you?"

"*You* mean something to me."

It takes a second for her expression to change from disbelief to pure, glorious glee. Then she's flinging her arms around me with a laugh that I can't help but return, throwing us back on the quilt.

Her lips press against mine, turning my laugh into a moan that escapes into her. It's a deep kiss. One I can't believe I'm having. I swear if she breaks from it now,

I'll be left with a wanting so deep, I'd search the desert to find it again. I run my thumb across her cheekbone. Brush my hand through her hair. Taste her tongue like it's the only meal I'll ever need.

I want her now—ache for how I had her last night—but I also want her just like this.

"I don't want to leave," she whispers.

I hold her face in my hands. "Then stay."

She smiles, pressing her cheek into my hand like it's her new favourite pillow. "I don't think this is how we should tell them about us."

A thrill runs through me at the word *us*. When have I ever been an *us*? "You're probably right." Come to think of it, how will Jordan react to this? Will he be happy that his sister has found someone? Or will he be pissed off because that person is me?

"What's the matter?" she asks, noticing the change on my face.

"Nothing." I take one last long look at her before dropping my hands. As she quietly disappears into the hall, my heart hammers like it wants to go with her.

I take a seat on my bed with a sigh that turns into a smile. I can't remember the last time I felt this way. I can't remember ever feeling this way—like there's a glow within me, chasing away all shadow.

Is this what Ophelia meant about the pain being

worth it? If it is, I think I might finally understand.

After a while, my sister pounds on the bathroom door, calling my name.

"I'm in here," I say, holding back my exasperation.

"Oh." She enters my room without knocking. No surprise there since my sister is a menace. "I thought I heard you go into the bathroom earlier."

"No. You heard Ophelia go into the bathroom."

"Oh," she says again, frowning as her eyes move to the quilt and pillows still strewn across the floor. "You slept on the floor?"

I try to keep my face as innocent-looking as possible. "The mattress was hurting my back."

"And you thought the floor would be better?"

No need to tell her that the floor was much, *much* better. "Is there a reason you're in here? Besides to annoy me?"

"Today's our last day."

I give her a second to elaborate. "So you're in here to point out the obvious?"

"No, stupid, I came in here to tell you we're eating out today. No point causing more mess when we need to be out early in the morning."

"I'll eat here." My heart thuds at the thought of getting to spend more time alone with Ophelia. "And I'll clean up after myself."

"Always having to complicate things." She shakes her head, leaving to bang on the bathroom door again. "Ophelia?"

"Yeah?" she calls over the sound of running water.

"We're eating out today so we don't make a mess. You in?"

"Okay! I'll come join you when I'm finished in the shower."

My insufferable sister gives me a look like she knows exactly what she's done to me. But that can't be true. If Evie knew I was only staying in because I wanted to spend more time with Ophelia, she'd be giving me worse looks than the one she's wearing now.

With my jeans pulled on, I wait until Ophelia unlocks the bathroom door before I spring into the hallway. She presses her back to the frame, cheeks flushed and hair wet, wearing only a towel.

I don't even think about it. Knowing that the other two are in their room, I take her face in my hands and kiss her. She reacts exactly how I would want her to—melting into me and kissing me back. Until she remembers that we aren't exactly in private. Feeling her tapping my arm, I step back, grinning at the look she's giving me. It's like she wants to reprimand me, but at the same time, she wants me to do it again.

"Stop smiling," she whispers, even though she's

smiling back. "You're so shameless." Shaking her head, she tightens her grip on her towel and darts to her bedroom, eyes lifting as she slowly closes her door.

Beautiful woman.

The smile stays on my face long after I finish showering. It continues all day. No matter how hard I try, I can't keep far away from her. When we're making coffee in the kitchen, I poke her ribs. When the sound of her ensuing laughter causes the other two to look over, I couldn't care less. I lift her by the waist when she can't reach a glass and plant her with kisses whenever we're alone.

"Right, let's go for breakfast." Evie throws me a suspicious look as I follow them to the door. "I thought you weren't coming?"

"I changed my mind." No way am I staying here while the girl I want to be with is out there.

Ophelia smirks as if she can read my mind, and I do my best to hide my smile as my sister continues to stare at me.

Honestly, as we step out into the fresh, chilly air, I'm already counting the seconds for this day to be over. I want to fast forward to when we're driving home, and it's just Ophelia and me in the car. Or better yet, when we're actually *at* home, inside a house where it's just the two of us making whatever noise we want.

For the first time in the entirety of my existence, I find myself jealous of my sister's romantic life. She gets to hold Jordan's hand in public, stroke his arm at the table, and give him kisses despite whether or not anyone is watching. I, on the other hand, have to resort to holding Ophelia's hand *beneath* the table. I have to kiss her cheek only when the other two are away.

The day drags slower than any of the others, but I guess that's what happens when you're waiting to be alone with someone. To make matters worse, the other two decide that because it's the last day, we should all stay up late. Not early so we can be alert for the drive home in the morning. *Late.*

My only solace is that Ophelia seems as displeased about it as I do.

She throws one unhappy look at me before smiling at Evie. "So, what do you want to play first?"

To push my frustration to its limits, my sister chooses the most time-consuming game on offer. She also seems determined to keep Ophelia away from me. She swaps teams so that I'm paired with Jordan, and when I offer to help Ophelia with the drinks, wanting a moment alone with her, Evie jumps up before I can push my chair away from the table.

I'm probably being paranoid. If my sister knew what was going on here—that I was serious about pursuing her—she wouldn't be hellbent on trying to destroy it. Right?

Or is that exactly what my sister is trying to do?

She's already warned me against making a move on her. But doesn't she realise how I must feel about her to be doing it?

With a deep, defeated sigh, I announce, "I'm going to bed."

Everyone stares at me.

"But we haven't finished the game," Evie complains.

"I don't mind playing as one," Jordan says. "If Adrian's tired, we shouldn't keep him up."

I don't look at Ophelia as I leave for my room. If I do, I might be inclined to stay, but I can already feel myself growing more frustrated with Evie. I know my sister warns every friend of hers away from me, and I'm only now starting to realise how little faith that means she has in me.

I'm dozing off when I hear my door softly open. Straining my eyes, I find Ophelia standing there, looking shy and perfect and like something I've conjured straight from a dream.

Wordlessly, I open the quilt for her to climb inside. She hesitates a second before doing so, her body moulding into mine as though I was created to fit around this one girl.

This one incredible fucking girl.

My dick is hard, but for the first time, I don't act on it. The last thing I want is for her to think that this is all she is to me—sex.

"I thought you weren't coming in here tonight," I say.

"I wasn't sure if you wanted me to."

I peer down at her. "You do realise that you make it a thousand times better by being here, right?"

She smiles and wraps her hands around my arm, holding me tight. "If only I came in here from that first night."

"Now that would have been a bit forward."

Laughing, she shuffles closer, resting her cheek against my chest in a way that has me holding my breath in a desperate need to freeze time. Taking her hand in mine, I contemplate how much has changed since the day we first arrived. It was just last week that I was dreading being here. Now here I am, with this girl in my arms, wishing to be no place else.

What is it about her that's made this change? Her warmth? Her quiet charm? Her ability to love through the deepest of pains? Whatever the reason, she has enraptured me thoroughly. There could be a meteor hurtling towards us, and I'd still make every futile attempt to save her.

With a sigh, I look at the ceiling. I don't know what

makes me think it, but from someplace deep within, one thought comes out. *You'd love her, Mum.*

"Will you be going back to work this week?" Ophelia murmurs.

I kiss her hand, feeling a pain that isn't exactly bad. "No. I'm not back until the New Year."

"What is it that you do again?" She nestles into the quilt as though settling in for a story.

"I'm a freelancer in online marketing," I answer. "I can work when and where I want, so I enjoy the freedom aspect of it. It's pretty good."

"And the job? Do you enjoy that aspect?"

"I do." I smile down at her, but all I can see is the faint outline of her shape in the dark. "What about you? You work in healthcare, right?"

"I do, but it's only temporary. I get to work when I want, too, which works really well for my plans. I want to go travelling."

"Travelling?" My brows raise. "You have a knack for adventure, Ophelia?"

"Yes, I have a knack for adventure, Adrian." I can hear the smirk in her voice. "How about you? Have you ever thought about travelling before?"

"I love travelling. It's one of the reasons I chose freelance. I'd just gotten back from Santo Domingo before I came here."

"Would you ever...go with someone else?"

The smile on my face may as well be a permanent fixture. "Is that your way of asking if I'd go with you?"

"Maybe." She's silent for a few seconds. "Does that scare you?"

"Not even a little bit." It surprises me how true that is. But the thought of getting on a plane with her—of jetting off to an island or a city or a farm in the middle of nowhere—is a thought I find exciting.

"That's good to know." She yawns, sleep on its way to claim her. "What's the favourite place you've visited?"

"Osaka. In Japan? I absolutely loved it there."

We talk into the night, even as she sounds sleepier and sleepier. We talk until I know she's no longer listening because she's no longer awake.

When I open my eyes in the morning, the sun hasn't quite risen, but Ophelia is no longer beside me. I stretch my arms out into a yawn, wishing for a morning when she doesn't have to disappear.

Because it's our last morning, it passes by in a blur. Everyone is racing to shower, racing to pack, racing to get out.

I load my bags into the back of my car before going inside to do a last-minute check. When I head back onto the deck, Ophelia is lugging her case down the drive.

"You can come with us this time," Evie calls from the

boot of her car just as I'm about to take Ophelia's case from her. "We have room for you."

Ophelia stills. I freeze with my hand on its way to her bag.

"Oh—um—I don't..." I feel Ophelia's eyes as they move to look up at me, but mine are on my sister, wondering if this is another attempt to keep Ophelia away from me or if I'm just being paranoid again.

"Why wouldn't you come with us?" Jordan asks, carrying his bags past us and dropping them in Evie's boot.

Again, I feel Ophelia's eyes on the side of my face, waiting for me to say something.

I straighten. "There's more room in my car. What's the point of you all cramping up inside one vehicle when she can come with me?"

"But you'd be going out of your way to take Phi," Jordan says matter-of-factly. "It made sense on the way here when we came before you, but it doesn't make sense now. You live out of town."

I hold back a sigh. How do I tell them that I wouldn't be going out of my way, not even a little bit, without tipping them off about how I feel?

I'd tell them about the two of us right now if I knew it was what Ophelia wanted. But I know what she'd say—that telling them right before a long drive home probably isn't the best timing. And she'd be right.

"It's fine," Ophelia concedes, barely holding back a sigh. "I'll go with Jordan and Evie, and we can all...meet when we get back."

The disappointment sits like an unwanted weight on my chest. But knowing that I'll get to see her again when we get back is all I need to hug my sister goodbye, shake Jordan's hand, and wrap my arms around Ophelia in an embrace that will always be a second too short.

Inside my car, I switch my ignition on and grip my steering wheel, waiting for Evie to leave first. She doesn't pull away from the drive. Instead, she leaves her car and walks over to me, indicating for me to roll my window down.

"Everything okay?" I ask.

"Everything's fine. I just..." She glances back at her car before lowering her face so it's levelled with mine. "I need to say this to you now rather than later. You and Ophelia..."

I struggle to keep my face straight. "Me and Ophelia?"

"There's something going on with the two of you, isn't there? Like...something more than casual?"

I debate lying, but that's something I've never liked doing with my sister. "I like her a lot, yeah."

Something undecipherable flickers across her face. But then she's frowning, and whatever she felt a moment ago is gone. "Please don't hurt her."

I flinch. "*That's* what you think of me?"

"You don't exactly have a good record with girls, Adrian."

So I wasn't being paranoid.

My eyes scan my sister's face, seeing, for the first time, what she truly thinks about me. "I've never intentionally hurt anyone, Evie. I just haven't found anyone that I want to be anything with. Until now."

Again, that undecipherable look that quickly morphs into something else. "It's not that I think you're going to intentionally hurt Ophelia. I know you won't. But I think there's a chance you're going to do it *un*intentionally. You've never had a girlfriend before. What if you get back home and realise it isn't something you want?"

I turn my face away.

"Adrian?"

"I know I want Ophelia," I say, still looking away from her. "Isn't that enough? I also know that I don't want to hurt her. Isn't *that* enough?"

"Not always." Evie sighs, and I start thinking...maybe she's right. Maybe I haven't thought this through properly. "All I'm saying is that you should use this drive home to think about it. That's it. And Adrian?" I force myself to look at her. "If you do really like her, I hope you make the right choice."

She walks back to her car. I watch as she climbs inside. Stare as she drives away.

How many times have I done this drive myself? How many times have I done it with a weight on my chest like it's an effort just to breathe? I thought it would be different this time—after all, it was different at the lodge—but as I drive, I feel the weight pressing in on me with each passing second, crushing me from angles I never knew to protect.

It's not just the thought of my mum anymore. It's the thought of the girl who's managed to sneak beneath the guard I've kept so diligently upheld.

What if Evie is right—what if I do end up hurting Ophelia? I don't want to hurt her. I know that. But what the hell do I know about treating someone right? I've spent my entire adult life keeping people at arm's length.

And Ophelia—what if she's the one who decides that I'm not who she wants? At the beginning of this trip, she still wanted her ex-boyfriend. Maybe in two weeks, she'll decide this was just a fling. An anomaly that she can't bear to continue.

She's been in love before. *Deeply* in love. What am I when compared to that?

Baggage. That's the only thing I carry. I'll spend the next year falling deeply in love with her only for her to realise that I'm not the one she wants to be with.

In the end, I'll end up losing her, too.

I slam my foot on the break as soon as I reach the nearest hard shoulder.

The feeling starts in my chest—a tightness that has me clutching the steering wheel and bracing myself for what I know is about to come.

Breathing becomes difficult. I take deep, painful rasps, but no matter how many times I try to suck in air, it doesn't seem to get further than my throat. My shirt feels too tight, the car too small.

Slamming my eyes closed, I try to remember everything I've learnt about panic attacks.

This will pass, I tell myself.

It will pass. It will pass. It will pass.

It has to pass.

CHAPTER SEVENTEEN

I stare at my phone like I can will the message to come.

How many times have I done that this week? How many seconds have I wasted wishing for something out of my control?

After we got home from the lodge a few days ago, I realised that I didn't have Adrian's number. Evie gave it to me without comment, and I messaged him that very night, foolish in my excitement. But with how we left things that morning, how could I not be excited? How could I not be certain that I'd awake in the morning to a message with sweet words and equal excitement?

My phone had no new messages in the morning. And three days later, I'm still waiting.

It's not like I'm demanding or needy or desperate or anything. I can usually go days without receiving a text back, and it won't faze me. But this is different. This is excitement turned into disappointment turned into confusion. Because why *wouldn't* he message me? I get that he might have been busy the first day—but the second—the third? Aren't you supposed to make an effort when you're interested in someone?

I don't even need to ask anyone to know the answer. Yes. Yes, you are. Which leads me to one conclusion—somewhere between then and now, he decided that he's no longer interested in me.

I hear a loud knock on my front door but don't bother moving from my bed to answer it. Whoever it is can leave me alone.

"Ophelia?" Evie calls, sounding as though she's shouting through the letterbox. It's followed by another loud knock. "Phi, are you home?"

I stuff my phone away and contemplate ignoring her. Really, I don't want to see or talk to anyone. But I also don't want to be this way, hiding away in my bedroom as the world makes plans without me.

"Phi?" she calls again, sounding worried this time.

Stuffing my phone into my joggers, I cave, heading downstairs and opening the door to find Evie wrapped up in a thick coat and scarf, shivering against the cold.

"You fixed your lock?" she asks, wiping her feet on the mat before stepping inside.

"No." I frown as I close the door after her. "I haven't fixed anything." I've barely even cleaned.

"Oh." She shrugs before removing her scarf and hanging it by the stairs. "It seems fixed to me."

I follow her into my living room, both loving the fact that she's comfortable enough to walk in herself and regretting that I'm not still alone in bed. "What brings you over?"

"I haven't heard from you since we got back." She takes a look around my living room before taking a seat. "I thought I'd come see you. Are you doing okay?"

I spare a second to wonder how I must look, given the fact that I haven't bothered to shower today. "I'm fine. I just...Holiday blues, I guess."

She runs her eyes over the room again. "You've made changes in here."

"Thought I should probably start adding some personality to this place." I sit beside her, playing with the fray of a new cushion. So far, all I've managed to do is add a few plants and home comforts, but it already feels better being in here.

"Any particular reason?"

I pause. The truth is that I've wanted to keep myself busy from the overwhelming urge to climb back into bed every time I get out of it. It's a feeling I hate—wanting to slump to the floor the second I exert a little energy. I'd felt this way a lot at the beginning of the year. Had caved to it, fought it, and then determined that I'd never feel that way away.

How has it come to me feeling this way again?

"You okay?" Evie asks.

I blink out of my thoughts, but they're still there, darkening a back corner of my mind. "I'm fine," I say with a smile. Part of me wants to admit the truth to her, to get it off my chest in the hopes that it'll help. But Adrian is her brother, and…I can't.

"He hasn't messaged you back, has he?"

I do a double-take. "What?"

"My brother. That's why you keep looking at your phone, isn't it?" I stare wordlessly at her, having not even realised I'd taken my phone out again. "Ophelia, I'm so sorry." She grabs my hand. "I knew something was going on between the two of you from how his mood changed whenever you came into the room. I thought he'd choose differently than this. I thought he'd get back and know for sure that he does want to try something with you. I didn't…Ophelia, you have to know that my brother has never been in a relationship before. I'm not sure commitment is something he can give. I'm sorry."

I reel from all of this new information, from Evie not

only knowing about Adrian and me but to the fact she's apologising for it on his behalf. "Have you—spoken to him about this yourself?"

She nods. Squeezes my hand. "I spoke to him before we left the lodge. At his car." I'd wondered what she was saying to him back then. I'd just assumed it was about the route home. Taking a deep breath, she continues, "I told him that he should use the car journey home to think about what he wants. That he shouldn't get into anything unless he's willing to commit. Not when it comes to you."

So is that what this is about? He's decided that he doesn't want us to go anywhere? We're a full stop after the lodge?

"Oh, Ophelia." Evie pulls me into a hug. "I truly am so sorry about this. I do know my brother has never liked anyone as much as you before. I know he's never been close to having anything with anyone but you before. But my brother...he's...complicated."

But that's the thing. I didn't think Adrian *was* complicated. Not since learning about his mum and his fear of losing someone like that again. To me, his love life—or lack of it—made sense after hearing that. But Evie doesn't know about those fears, does she? She just thinks he's bad at relationships.

He isn't afraid of commitment. He's afraid of losing

the people he loves.

I stare at a spot on my carpet.

For the first time since returning, I think about Adrian, alone in his car, driving back from the lodge with only his thoughts for company. Has he convinced himself that he's going to lose me, so he's stopped this before we can begin?

But we've already begun. The butterflies have started, the memories created. We've shared a kiss, we've shared a bed. I've told him things about myself that I haven't told anyone else, and he's done the same with me.

He might have decided that this is over, but I'm not letting us go without a fight.

"You said Adrian will be at the New Year's Eve event, right?" I ask.

"Yeah...?"

"Can I still buy a ticket?"

*

I pull at the skirt of my satin black dress as I reach the venue. I can hear the music booming from within, mingled with the voices of the people waiting to get inside. I feel severely overdressed, which is silly, considering there are girls here dressed in far nicer things than me.

As I join the queue, I start regretting my decision to make this journey alone. I could have caught the train with my brother and Evie—who assured me that Adrian was going separately with a group of his friends—but at the mention of his name, I suddenly wanted to do this solitary.

Being alone, I thought, would give me time to prepare. Or, at the very least, the freedom to turn around if I changed my mind. I haven't changed my mind. I am doing this, fear be damned. But...It would be nice to have someone to walk inside with. To have them hold my hand and preferably do the talking for me.

I show security my ticket and take a deep breath, remembering all the embarrassing things I said to Adrian at the lodge and how I can't possibly embarrass myself more in front of him. It still doesn't stop my nerves from kicking up a notch as I step inside, but I place one foot in front of the other, determined to beat them.

The party is already in full swing. I can blame myself for that. I might be here, but I did allow two trains to pass before I finally got the courage to get on one.

There are two floors. I hand my coat in on the first and receive a complimentary glass of champagne. Feeling exposed in my thin black straps, I accept a second glass when one of the hosts sees that I'm shaking and takes pity on me.

I head downstairs—to where the real party is—and

scan every place my eyes can see. The right side of the room holds a dancefloor, while the left has a fancy bar where most people seem to be mingling. There's also an outside terrace where a lot of noise is coming from. I check indoors first, but I don't find Adrian. I do spot Jordan and Evie by the bar, chatting with some of their friends, but I decide to keep my arrival unknown to them, at least for now.

Stepping outside, I ignore the chill and try not to think about what I'll do when I actually find Adrian. I remind myself that I'm a grown-ass woman who can hold her own, and this is not how he gets to end things with me.

A group of boys call me over. I ignore them and wish I'd kept my jacket.

The further down I get, the less faith I have that Adrian is even here.

Until I hear a voice that I recognise as distinctly his.

I take a few steps back. The table I'd dismissed so easily is the one where I now find him. He has a girl draped over his lap—hence why I'd dismissed the table. I wasn't looking for this. I never would have looked for this.

I watch as she whispers something in his ear, listen as he laughs. Envy, sharp and hideous, stabs my chest. If I wanted to run away now, I wouldn't be able to. Something is pinning me here. Something is smothering the candle I'd kept burning for him.

Hope is a treacherous thing. It's what brought me this far. It's what made me think that, despite everything, despite his days of silence, Adrian was thinking about me like I was him. How could he not be? The days we'd spent together at the lodge were intense. They were real. They took us from two strangers to something more. Or is it out of sight, out of mind for him? Is a few days all it takes for him to push me to the back of his thoughts and forget?

"Hey, there," someone at the table says to me. "And who are you?"

I look away from Adrian to find one of his friends smiling at me. He's obviously interested, and for a second, I imagine myself getting revenge on Adrian by flirting with him. But I won't stoop to his level. I won't put hurt out into the world because it's been given to me.

"I'm Ophelia," I say, giving one last look to Adrian. "And I'm leaving."

Upon hearing my name, his eyes shoot over, and I'm satisfied to at least see his smile fade as quickly as the colour drains from his cheeks.

I waste no more seconds watching him.

"Ophelia, wait!"

I hear his voice behind me, followed by a noise like

someone trying to shove a heavy table out of the way, but I don't stop moving.

A hand catches mine. "Ophelia, please."

How many times has his hand made me feel something by simply touching me?

Taking a deep breath, I give in trying to walk away and turn to face him, heart softening at the concern etched deep behind his eyes. "Yes?"

His eyes scan my face. The same blue that welcomed me into morning just a few days ago with a smile that convinced me I'd meant something. "What are you doing here?"

"What am I—?" I pull my hand from his, clenching it by my side. "I'm here because you haven't spoken to me since the lodge. I'm here because I wanted to speak to you in person."

"About what?"

"About..." Now my eyes scan his face. Is he really going to pretend like he doesn't know what's going on here? "About the fact that you haven't spoken to me since leaving the lodge. The way we left things...I don't understand."

"What—you didn't think things would be the same between us after leaving, did you?"

I flinch. But the concern that was in his eyes moments ago has now gone, replaced by something hard—and cold.

"Yes," I breathe. "Yes, that is what I thought. And why wouldn't I?" I demand, unamused by his downplay. "You gave me every reason to think that, Adrian. Or are you going to deny that?"

No warmth re-enters his eyes as he says the words to me. "We had a good few days. I admit that. But that's all it was—a good few days."

"Right." I look over his shoulder at the girl he had draped over his lap. "Because you've found someone better now?"

His jaw works. "Don't pretend like you don't have someone better than me."

"What's that supposed to mean?"

"Your ex-boyfriend? You'd drop me the second he came back."

"Do you want to know what I think?" I can feel my eyes watering, but I force the tears to wait. "I think you're afraid. I think you're scared of starting something with me because you don't know how it will end. I get it, and I don't blame you. I can't make you think that we're worth it, Adrian. All I can do is tell you that *I* think we are. And I'm not going anywhere. *You're* the one I haven't been able to stop thinking about since the first day we met. Not anyone else."

His throat bobs. The only sign to tell me he's feeling

anything. But then I see it—the moment he rebuilds his walls, shutting me out again. "You don't know me, Ophelia. So don't pretend like you do. I'm not doing this because I'm afraid. I'm doing this because I've decided I don't want anything more with you."

His words sting. They claw up my chest until I'm almost choking on them. But still, I don't believe him.

Aren't lies so easily spoken? Capable of inflicting pain as though they're the truth. But what they can't do is rewrite memories. They can't take away the moments we shared or the belief in my heart that he wants something more with me. That man who'd held me in his arms a few days ago—the man who'd told me I meant something to him—he still exists.

But I've hoped before, and I've believed before, and I've come away empty-handed.

"You have two choices," I tell him. "You can either come back with me, or you can stay and continue whatever intentions you have with that girl over there. Because I'm not being the only one to fight for this. I'm not being the only one to hold on. You have to meet me halfway." I give him a few seconds to make up his mind. When he doesn't say or do anything, I take that as his decision. "Alright."

I turn.

I swear I see his face crumble as I do.

But he doesn't do anything to stop me.

And he doesn't call me back.

*

My brother sits quietly on the edge of my bed, watching as I throw clothes into a suitcase. I know he has something to say to me, but I don't have it in me to ask him what it is.

"What day do you fly again?"

Knowing that wasn't the question he wanted to ask, I still answer, "Saturday."

It's been two weeks since New Year's Eve. Two weeks, but a few days is all it took for me to finally decide to get out there and stop holding myself back for people who are content on letting me go on without them.

I want to travel the world. I want to see all the beautiful places I've only daydreamed about until now. I wanted to do this years ago, but there's always been something holding me back. Work. Saving for a mortgage. Being part of a two. Yet I've been single for almost a year, and I still haven't made the move. It's time to admit to myself that the only reason for that is me.

I'm the one who's afraid.

I'm the one holding myself back.

My brother makes a heavy breathing noise, and I finally crack. "Whatever it is you have to say to me, you can say it."

"This is because of Adrian, isn't it?"

A beat.

"No," I answer, folding a dress and placing it with my others. "I'm doing this for me."

"I know that there's something going on between the two of you. Why didn't you tell me about it yourself?"

"I guess I didn't need to this time." I look up at him with a smile that I mean. "I thought I had something with him, but it turns out I don't. I'm okay with it. I'm moving on."

His eyes scan my face. "He was the one who fixed the lock on your door, by the way."

"My lock?"

"When we got back from the lodge, the first thing that Adrian did was fix your lock. He told me that he'd been tossing and turning all night thinking about how easily he got in. He cares about you."

I swallow a lump in my throat. Hope threatens to resurface, flickering in my chest like an eternal flame, but there's a reason why Adrian chose not to tell me this himself. Why he isn't here now. "It doesn't matter. I'm not sure how much Evie told you, but Adrian had a whole car journey to decide if he wanted to start something with me. He decided he didn't."

"It wasn't Evie who told me about the two of you. It was Adrian."

My head whips back towards him. "What? When? Why?"

Jordan shifts on the bed. "I saw him. On New Year's Eve. I've never seen him looking so beaten, Phi. He was sitting alone outside. He told me he'd seen you, and when I asked him why that would upset him, he told me the rest. He's fallen for you, Phi. He's just too afraid to do anything about it."

I slump down on the bed beside him. "That's exactly what I thought. But what use is that to me?"

"What do you mean?"

"He isn't here now, is he? He hasn't messaged me since leaving the lodge, has he? You say he's fallen for me, but where's the proof? Better yet, what has it given to me?" I can tell he's about to say something in Adrian's defence, so I hold up my hands. "I know. I know that this is hard for Adrian. I know that he's never experienced this with a girl before. But how many times do I have to wait around for somebody to decide I'm worth fighting for?"

Jordan is silent for a moment. "You're not just talking about Adrian, are you?"

"No," I sigh. "I've waited once before, as you already know. I don't think I can do it again."

"I get it." He places a hand on my shoulder. "But what I will say is that I think you and Adrian could be good together. Happy. There's something about you both that just...works."

"It can only work if we both want it to."

He tilts his head. "Do you want to know what I admire the most about you? What I didn't realise until your breakup? You're a fighter, Phi. More so than anyone else I know. You fight even if the probability isn't on your side. And if there's a chance you'll end up hurt, you fight anyway. Don't you think you and Adrian are worth fighting for, too?"

My brows pull together. My brother is right. I have always fought. I've always given my absolute everything for the people I think are worth it because even if I've lost, I've at least known I did all I could.

But...why does this have to be a fight?

"The thing is," I say, clearing my throat to get the words out louder, "I *do* think we're worth it. But the problem here is that Adrian doesn't. And I don't want to be the one who fights anymore. I want to be the one someone fights for. I want someone to look at me and know I'm worth it without me having to show them. I want to be happy, Jordan. And right now, what will make me happy is going out into the world and choosing myself." A tear falls onto my lap. I wipe my eyes, feeling a new fight burning within me. A fight for *me*.

Jordan is silent for a few moments. After a deep sigh,

he takes my hand and says, "Then I think you should be getting on that flight, and I think you should be waiting for no one."

CHAPTER EIGHTEEN

Adrian

"You're making a mistake."

Evie has said this multiple times already. It's like she isn't aware of the hole eroding away in my chest, screaming *mistake* at me every painful second.

But what's done is done. By now, Ophelia will be heading to the airport, and I'll be left as a small part of her past, a mere blot that she'll barely remember.

"Please," Evie starts again, "tell me why you're doing this." She grips my arm. "I know I told you to think about it on your drive home, but I didn't think you'd choose the option that's clearly making you miserable."

"I'm not miserable."

"He says without a single smile shown in days."

I sigh, looking down at my hands. "What does it matter, anyway? She'll be on her flight soon. I'm not going to be the one to stop her." How could I? How can I even look at her after all the lies I told her on New Year's Eve? I don't want anything more with her being the biggest one.

"Who said anything about stopping her? She deserves to know how you feel so she can make the decision herself."

"What's the point?"

"*A-dri-an.*" She shakes my arm as she says each syllable. "The point is that she could be The One for you. The point is that when you're with her, you're happy, and when she's with you, she's happy. The point is happiness, Adrian!"

"She'll find happiness without me. And I—And I—" A future without Ophelia. A future without even getting to call her a friend. How can I face that after glimpsing what life is like with her in it?

"Is this all because you don't think you deserve to be happy?" Evie sounds as if she's trying really hard to understand why I'm doing this. I turn my face away, wondering if there's any reason that would make sense. "Is that what this is?" She grips my hand. "Because you do, Adrian. You're the best man I've ever met, and Ophelia is the best woman. I can't think of a better match than the two of you."

I wipe my eyes before a tear can slip out. "It's not that I don't think I deserve to be happy. It's that—" I swallow. "It's that—I'm afraid of it. I'm afraid of losing her like—like we lost mum."

Evie is silent for several seconds. Although I'm relieved to have gotten that off my chest to her, I can't bear to look at her.

After a while, she says, "Isn't it ironic that in your fear of losing her, you're losing her?"

"At least it doesn't hurt this way."

She wipes a rogue tear from my cheek. One that's managed to escape. "Doesn't hurt? Can you honestly tell me that you aren't hurting right now?" More tears threaten to fall. I do all I can to fight them back. "You can't live like this, Adrian. You can't live with the fear of death hanging over you."

"Then how do I make it stop?"

"You live." She takes my hand again. "I know that grieving the loss of someone you love is the worst kind of pain, but death is part of life, *losing* someone is part of life, and it isn't the only type of grief you can experience. There's also the grief for a love you might have had if you'd made different choices. Right now, you're afraid of a future that hasn't happened and a past that you can't change. That isn't living, Adrian."

I have no words for her. All I have is this hole that continues to erode.

"I know you're afraid of losing Ophelia," she continues. "But regardless of your fear, she's going to die one day, just like the rest of us. Don't you want to make sure that she spends every day laughing and smiling? Don't you want to be her shoulder to cry on and another reason she has for breathing? If she has no one else, don't you want her to have you? Ophelia likes you. I know you think it's nothing and she'll easily move on, but Ophelia falling for anyone is no easy feat. She's fallen for exactly two people in her entire life. You're one of them. And you're losing her by sitting here talking to me."

I wipe my eyes with the sleeve of my sweater. Evie is wrong about one thing...I don't think Ophelia liking me is nothing. I think it's the biggest honour of my life having her even look at me in that way. But that's where my problem stems from. I'm the man who stands to lose her.

Yet...she's also right about the other thing. I'm losing her anyway. The only difference is that this way, I'm losing her by choice. Why the fuck would I *choose* to lose her?

"I'm making a huge mistake, aren't I?"

Evie's laugh is of pure relief. "It isn't too late to change that." She taps my phone. "Call her."

"I can't do this over the phone." I'd freeze the second she answers. That's if she even does after all I said to her.

"Then what are you still doing here?" Evie jumps to her feet. "Go to her!"

I jump to my feet with her, unsure about my next move. "What if I'm too late?"

"You won't know unless you go."

"What if she's already gotten through security?"

"Buy yourself a plane ticket and get through security with her!"

I chuck her my car keys on my way to the door.

"What are these for?" she asks, staring at them in puzzlement.

"You're coming with me. I need you to drive while I book a flight."

"We're actually doing this." Suddenly, Evie is as frantic as me, and together, we're racing to my car like two maniacs about to miss the biggest meeting of their lives. "Okay," Evie breathes. "Have you got your seatbelt on?"

"I've got my seatbelt on."

"Then let's not waste another second."

She drives. I book onto the first flight I find, one leaving today, checking in and praying that I don't miss Ophelia.

I'm not sure how I feel about any of this. Last year, I was certain that I'd be alone forever. Now I'm on my way to tell the girl I'm pretty sure is the love of my life that she's worth any amount of pain coming my way. Of course she is. How could I have ever thought otherwise?

"You're fidgeting," Evie says.

"I know." I don't stop moving my leg as she drives up the motorway, grumbling about what a pain in the ass it is to be driving such a big car. "I'll buy you a meal for this," I tell her.

"Are you kidding me?" Both her hands grip the wheel. "You don't have to buy me anything. It's enough to be a part of this."

I jump out of the car as she goes to find a parking spot. I'm more nervous than I've ever been in my life, but there isn't enough time to waste on it.

Having no bag with me, I expect to fly through security, but there's still a queue to get behind. I wait with the patience of somebody first practising it. Once through, I race to the board that announces gate numbers, finding Ophelia's already boarding.

I run. There's nothing else for it. Nothing to stop my heart from pound-pound-pounding like it has a race to win. If Ophelia has already boarded that plane…but I won't think about it. I can't.

When I finally reach her gate, I see a small queue of

people still waiting to board, but no Ophelia. I race down the line, checking every face, but I already know that it's no use. She isn't here.

"Excuse me," I pant, stopping by the flight attendant's desk. "There's a girl on the plane I need to speak to. Can you please—*please*—help me find her?"

"I'm sorry, sir, but if you could please get to the back of the line, I'll help you once you show me your boarding pass."

"I don't have a boarding pass."

"Then I'm afraid I can't help you."

"I don't have a boarding pass because I'm not on this flight, but the girl I need to speak to is. It'll just be for a moment. Can you please let me through to find her?"

I feel like an idiot. Obviously, there's no chance she's letting me through without a boarding pass, yet here I am, begging her like I'm not wasting our time.

"Without a boarding pass, I can't let you through. I'm sorry, but that's the rule."

"Not even if you escort me back here yourself?"

She must see the frantic look on my face because she seems to deliberate. But then she's shaking her head again. "I'm sorry. Truly. Maybe you can speak to her after she lands."

"Yeah. Thanks anyway." I turn, defeated, wishing there was a seat left on *this* flight so I could pay any amount of money to take it.

That's when I see her.

A girl with her head down, sitting in the corner farthest away from where I'm standing.

Is it …?

"Ophelia?"

She looks up, and something I can't put into words happens inside of me when her hazel eyes meet mine. "Adrian?" She gets to her feet. Steps towards me. I step towards her. "What are you doing here?"

"I came to find you." When I reach her, I take her face in my hands, if only to make sure she's real. Am I really lucky enough to have not missed this chance with her? "I have some things to say."

Her eyes are so beautiful in their expressiveness. I can see the way they work, flickering between surprise, hope, confusion, and back to hope again. "What things?"

I tuck a strand of hair behind her ears. "Well, for starters, I'm sorry for being a massive asshole to you after leaving the lodge."

"Oh." She huffs out a laugh. "That."

I grin. "Yeah. That."

Now she smiles. "Thank you for apologising for it. Anything else?"

"Well," I lower my hands to take hold of hers, rubbing

my thumbs across her knuckles. "I've come to realise some things. Some very important things." Exhaling slowly, I meet her eyes. "On my drive home from the lodge, I had a panic attack. I'm fine," I quickly assure her. "I just want you to know the full story. I've fallen for you, Ophelia. Hard. And because I've never allowed it to happen before, I haven't known how to deal with it. I felt so happy being with you that when I wasn't, I worked myself up into a frenzy thinking about all the ways it could go wrong. I'm afraid of losing you, and because of that, I pushed you away. I've focused so much on what might happen in the future that I forgot to appreciate what I have now. You. Here. Holding my hands."

I smile again. "I want to be the one who gets to do this. I want to be the one to hold you every night as you fall asleep. I want to see you smile every morning and hear your laugh every day. I want to confide in you about my problems and comfort you when you have your own. I want to learn all there is to know about you, from what makes you tick to what makes you jump up and down in excitement. And if pain eventually comes from having all of that..." I look down as I entwine our fingers together. "Well, you're worth it. Ophelia, you're worth risking my heart for."

"Adrian..."

I look up at her, but before either of us can say

anything else, we hear an announcement overhead, notifying us that Ophelia's gate will soon close.

"Wait a second." I search her face as I realise something. "Why aren't you on your flight?"

A slow smile spreads across her face. "Well...You aren't the only one to realise something." She takes my face in her hands. "I'm a fighter, Adrian. And I'd fight for you."

A fire soars up my chest, scorching me in a way that forges me to her. I want to take her in my arms. I want to kiss her and worship her and do a thousand other things that wouldn't be appropriate here. But—

"You need to get on this flight."

She frowns. "What?"

Gently lowering her hands, I say, "Ophelia, this has been a dream of yours for too long. You're so close to seeing the world, and I don't want to be the one to stop you."

"But how can I leave now? How can I go after—after—after *this*?" She shakes her head with a panic I can see building. "I don't want to spend three months without you. I don't. I won't."

I press my lips to her forehead. Now who's being frantic? "The world can't keep waiting for you, love. But I can. Besides, I can work from wherever I want. Remember? Give me two weeks to get things sorted, and

I'll fly to wherever you are in this world. Trust me. I don't want to spend three months without you, either."

"But what if you change your mind? What if time passes and you get scared again, and you realise I'm not what you want?"

A cloud of sadness strays over to me. All this time, I've been thinking about my fears. It never occurred to me that I'm not the only one afraid of losing something. And I haven't given her much reason to be confident I'll stay.

"You won't know until you go, will you?" I squeeze her hands. "But I'll prove to you that I won't run away again. I'll be on that flight, all in. And if I'm not..." My shoulders rise and fall. "You can laugh at the idiot who let the best woman he's ever met go."

She smiles. "I suppose I can have a lot of fun in those two weeks alone."

I quirk a brow. "I think you'll find that the fun starts when I arrive."

She glances over my shoulder at the boarding desk, but I have one more thing to say to her. "I know that you were deeply in love with your ex-boyfriend. I know that when we first met, you told me that your heart still beats for him. But I promise you now that I'm going to do all I can to deserve having it beat for me."

She squeezes my hands. "It doesn't matter who came

before you. What matters is that, from now on, you're the one I choose." A last-call announcement has her looking over my shoulder again. "I guess I should go..."

My chest pangs at the thought of her being so far away from me, but I say, "I guess I should move out of your way."

She holds my eyes as she walks around me, gripping my hands until our arms are outstretched.

I tug her back. "You didn't think I was letting you go without one of these, did you?" Crushing my lips to hers, I kiss her with a force that could shatter a thousand planets or burst a thousand stars. "I'll be on that flight," I murmur as I lean my forehead against hers.

She smiles against me. "I'll be waiting."

Epilogue

A warm breeze ruffles my hair, pulling a pleased sigh from my lips. My eyes are closed. They don't need to be open for me to know that the sky is clear—as blue and as beautiful as the day we arrived.

My head rests against Adrian's thigh, my new favourite place. His quick fingers move across his keyboard as the waves make a gentle *whooshing* noise behind us on the quiet, golden sands we hiked all morning to find. It sounds like peace and solitude and utter bliss.

When I first saw Adrian wheeling his luggage through those airport doors all those weeks ago, my heart jumped in a way that I never thought it would again. Not everyone is lucky enough to get a second chance at an epic love. Yet as I lay here on this beautiful island with the feel of Adrian beneath me, his warmth more bliss than the heat of the sun, that's how this feels. Epic.

A finger touches my lips, and I open my eyes to find Adrian watching me, the blue of his eyes more stunning than the sky. "What's this smile for?" he asks.

This is a game we like to play: what causes this smile, and how can I make it happen again?

"Aren't you supposed to be working?" I ask.

He smirks and leans his head back against the tree he's using for support, his skin sun-kissed and his hair matted in a way that's far too sexy. "I am working. I'm trying to figure out what this smile is for." He touches my lips again.

"I'm smiling because of where I am and who I'm with," I answer.

His smile widens. "I'm smiling for the same reason."

I sit up, twisting to rest my chin on his shoulder. "Thank you for joining me here." For the first few days, I'll admit that I feared he wouldn't. "I know it isn't easy opening yourself up like this, but besides this beautiful, stunning, incredible place we've found ourselves in, you're the reason I'm happy."

He brushes my hair behind my ear, eyeing my face with sudden seriousness. "I've been wondering something, and I'd love to hear what you think about it."

"Go on."

"Is it possible to love someone after so short amount of time?"

My stomach flips. But— "I don't think so," I answer honestly. His brows flick up, and not wanting to hurt him, I explain, "But I do think it's possible to know if you're going to love them." As I look into his beautiful face, I wonder if it is possible, after all, to love someone so soon. That's what this feels like. But I want to get to know him first. I want to fall in love with every part of him, from how he takes his coffee in the morning to how he handles his mistakes. Because he'll make them—just like I will. But isn't that what love is?

Love isn't an idea. It's flesh and bones and a beating heart. It's choices and actions and words that are said and words that are left unspoken. It's releasing control. It's placing trust in another and making damn sure they can trust you in return. It's learning and growing and arguing and forgiving. It's accepting that you aren't two halves of one whole. You're two wholes choosing to be together. It's knowing that one day this person might have to leave you, and if that day ever comes, you'll honour them by feeling every ounce of pain that comes your way.

Adrian takes my hands in his. "I'm going to love you, Ophelia Jones."

I smile as I say the words back to him, feeling their truth from the depths of my heart. "And I'm going to love you, too, Adrian Wilde. So let's meet each other halfway."

AFTERWORD

If you enjoyed reading this book, please consider leaving it a review. It is a huge help to self-published authors!

PLAYLIST

The Lumineers - *Ophelia*

Matt Schuster - *Ophelia*

Beyoncé - *XO*

Taylor Swift - *Daylight*

Taylor Swift - *Safe & Sound*

Taylor Swift - *loml*

Benson Boone - *Beautiful Things*

Printed in Great Britain
by Amazon